RISING

A Post-Apocalyptic/Dystopian Adventure

The Traveler Series Book Four

Tom Abrahams

A PITON PRESS BOOK

RISING

© 2017 by Tom Abrahams
All Rights Reserved

Cover Design by Hristo Kovatliev
Edited by Felicia A. Sullivan
Proofread by Pauline Nolet
Proofread by Patricia Wilson
Interior design by Stef McDaid at WriteIntoPrint.com

This book is a work of fiction. People, places, events, and situations are the product of the author's imagination.

Any resemblance to actual persons, living or dead, or historical events is purely coincidental.

No part of this book may be reproduced, stored in a retrieval system, or transmitted by any means without the written permission of the author and publisher.

tomabrahamsbooks.com

FREE PREFERRED READERS CLUB: Sign up for information on discounts, events, and release dates:

eepurl.com/bWCRQ5

Works by Tom Abrahams

THE TRAVELER
POST APOCALYPTIC/DYSTOPIAN SERIES
HOME
CANYON
WALL
RISING
BATTLE (LATE 2017)

THE SPACEMAN CHRONICLES
POST-APOCALYPTIC THRILLERS
SPACEMAN
DESCENT
RETROGRADE

PERSEID COLLAPSE: PILGRIMAGE SERIES NOVELLAS
CROSSING
REFUGE
ADVENT

RED LINE: AN EXTINCTION CYCLE NOVEL

MATTI HARROLD POLITICAL CONSPIRACIES
SEDITION
INTENTION

JACKSON QUICK ADVENTURES
ALLEGIANCE
ALLEGIANCE BURNED
HIDDEN ALLEGIANCE

For Courtney, Sam, Luke, and the nation of Finland

*"Victorious warriors win first and then go to war,
while defeated warriors go to war first and then seek to win."*

—Sun Tzu

Chapter 1

SEPTEMBER 30, 2042, 9:07 AM
SCOURGE +10 YEARS
EAST OF RISING STAR, TEXAS

He heard the scream first. Then the unmistakable pop of rifle shots crackled through the still West Texas air.

Lola!

Marcus Battle sprang to his feet and sprinted from the garden, drawing his Glock from his hip holster on the run.

Another bloodcurdling scream pierced his ears and traveled down his spine as he rounded the side of the barn and a body flopped from the treehouse to the ground.

His finger was on the trigger, his head up, his eyes scanning the overgrown, waist-high grass. To the right, beyond the treehouse, was a man on a horse. Marcus crouched low, sprinting straight at the man, rushing through the grass, the long blades slapping against his body and his face as he moved with purpose to the stranger.

Behind him there was a trio of muffled shots, but Marcus ignored them. One threat at a time. He resisted the urge to call for Lola, Sawyer, or little Penny. That wouldn't help them and it would give away his position to whoever else was with the man on the horse.

He reached the treehouse and used the thick, aging trunk as cover from the man on horseback. With his back pressed against the tree, he slid his butt to his heels and curled from one side to the other, searching the ground for the body that fell from the house above.

He'd circled nearly three-quarters of the trunk when he saw Sawyer's twisted body. Battle grit his teeth and closed his eyes, resisting the urge to scream. He lowered himself onto his stomach and used a military crawl to inch closer to his adopted son. Sawyer's face was turned away from Marcus, his worn denim jacket shrugged high on his back. There was a compound fracture torn through his pants. Marcus reached his trembling hand to the boy and touched his back, then slid his hand to Sawyer's neck. He pulled his hand away and balled it into a fist.

Marcus rolled away from Sawyer and inched himself up against the bark. Once on his feet, he maneuvered under cover toward the man on horseback. He got to within twenty yards. The man on the horse was more a boy, a fresh-faced and wide-eyed lookout. His rifle rested across the front of his saddle.

Marcus inched closer and then stood above the grass, the Glock leveled at the boy. "Don't do it," he said when the boy struggled with his weapon. "Raise your hands and start talking."

The boy's mouth dropped open, but he said nothing. He raised his trembling hands above his head. The rifle teetered and slid to the ground.

"How many?" Marcus said.

The boy shook his head.

Marcus squeezed the trigger and winged the boy's shoulder. "How many?"

The horse backed up but didn't spook. The boy grabbed his shoulder, tears welling in his eyes, and stuttered, "F-five."

Marcus looked past the boy toward the highway. At the edge of the road he could see a team of horses near his fence. He stepped closer, tightened his grip on the Glock, and pulled the trigger again. The bullet struck the boy in the other arm, rendering him useless.

Marcus bridged the distance to the horse and picked up the boy's rifle, an FDE brown AR-10.

With one hand, he clumsily aimed the rifle at the boy's chest. "You keep quiet," he said. "Not a sound. You understand?"

The boy nodded, his teeth digging into his bottom lip and tears streaking down his face. Marcus holstered his Glock and bolted back toward the house.

Marcus tried remembering where the rest of his family was. Lola was in the garage when he'd gone out to tend the garden. Penny was asleep in the barn.

As he moved back toward the house, cutting across the yard, he caught a flash of movement to his right. He spun. A pair of men were leaving the garage. Marcus pressed the rifle against his shoulder, drew his eye to the scope, aimed, and squeezed the trigger twice.

Twin bursts sliced through the air and a spray of crimson burst from one man's head. Marcus inched to the left and pressed the trigger again. Another two pops caught the second man in his neck and chest. Both dropped beneath the tall grass.

Battle kept the scope to his eye and scanned to the left. No targets. He lowered the AR-10 and raced to the garage. He almost tripped over the men he'd felled. One had a knife at his side. The other was armed with a pistol tucked into the front of his rope-cinched waistband.

He sidestepped them and reached the garage door, shouldering his way into the open space. He'd constructed a kitchenette in the garage, running the workable plumbing and gas lines from the no-longer-standing main house. He'd scavenged the appliances from neighboring abandoned properties over the past five years.

The lights were off and only the dim cracks of morning light seeped through the frayed wall joints of the aluminum building. The hair on Marcus's neck stood on end. He sensed something sinister awaited him.

He thumbed the holster open and silently withdrew the Glock, moving cautiously through the gray-lit space. The kitchen was on the opposite end, closest to where the house had stood.

His eyes adjusted to the darkness and he could make out the shapes of the small refrigerator and gas cooktop built atop cinder blocks. He didn't see Lola until he was feet from her.

She was facedown, a pool of blood collecting around her upper torso. Her T-shirt was torn from her bare back and one leg was twisted at an odd angle.

Swallowing a thick knot bulging in his throat, Marcus knelt beside her and gently touched the back of her head. He pulled his hand away bloodied.

"Lola?" he croaked.

He placed his red-soaked hand on her back and closed his eyes. She wasn't breathing. Marcus pulled the AR-10 from his shoulder and set it on the concrete beside him.

He reached over and, using her shoulders, rolled her onto her side. He winced and looked away. His eyes were closed, but still he could see her dead eyes looking back at him.

Marcus clenched his jaw. His throat burned. He laid her facedown in the position he'd found her, picked up the rifle, holding it by the hand guard and the pistol grip, and marched heavily toward the garage exit. His boots slapped against the concrete in rhythm until he burst through the open doorway. The sunlight blinded him for an instant and he squatted beneath the blades of grass and clumps of bull thistle.

His eyes adjusted and he worked his way to his right, back to the barn. If the boy on the horse wasn't lying, there were three men left to kill. He had to find them before they hurt Penny.

Marcus bounded through the grass, which he'd let grow uncontrolled to make it more difficult for anyone to find them. He wanted his property to look abandoned. For five years it had worked. Somehow these monsters had found them.

Marcus looked to his left as he ran. The boy on the horse was gone. Marcus immediately regretted not killing him. He'd shown mercy to a child. Unless infection got to him, it was a mistake. He could feel it in his gut.

He reached the edge of the barn and used its corner as cover. He checked the rifle and pulled it to his shoulder, pressing its stock tightly against his shoulder. He moved stealthily toward the entrance, his ears pricked for anything that might give away the intruders' positions, but heard nothing.

The door was cracked. Marcus backed away from it and in one motion leapt forward, kicked it open, and threw his body into the barn, his finger on the trigger.

The lights were on in the building they used as their home. Directly across from Marcus, stretching across the wall opposite the entrance, were large storage racks. They were only a quarter full, but an intruder was helping himself. As he targeted the red-bearded man stuffing bags and cans into a burlap sack, a loud pop echoed from his left near the deep freezer. Before Marcus reacted, a slug slammed into his body. Despite the searing heat of the shot, he still tightened his finger on the trigger and pulled, leveling a trio of shots at the red-bearded man. He missed and instead hit a large package of toilet paper, which exploded in a cloud of white paper shrapnel.

Another pop echoed from the right where Marcus stored what was left of his arsenal. Instantly, he bent against the heavy punch of another shot. The shock of the hit knocked him off-balance and he dropped the rifle, the sling catching on his forearm before the weapon rattled harmlessly to the floor.

Marcus reached for his holster, struggling to find the Glock's grip, as another shot pierced his flesh, bringing with it a searing heat that forced a guttural moan from his aching throat.

Marcus dropped to his knees and worked hard to focus on the trio of men converging on him. Straight ahead, the sneering red-bearded man approached. He was armed with a pair of handguns and two-fisted them like he was a slinger from the Old West. On the backs of his hands were identical black ink tattoos of dollar signs.

Sucking in each breath with more difficulty, Marcus braced himself with his hands. He reached for his hip and the Glock, but couldn't manage the strength to free it. From the left he heard a deep, resonant chuckle. He looked up to see a short, squatty man with a patch over his right eye, a rifle over his shoulder. His teeth were yellow and his lips curled around them like a pair of mating slugs. The man reached over and took the handgun, tossing it across the garage floor toward the shelving on the opposite wall.

"It's not turning out to be the kind of day you expected, now is it?" the man with the patch asked.

"His *last* day," came a thickly accented voice from the right. "And he won't even make it to lunch." The Southern drawl was unmistakably Texas.

Marcus dropped his head and glanced to his right in time to see a man with a long scar running the length of his angular face squat in front of him. The man kicked away the rifle, reached out with a gloved hand, and touched the side of Marcus's face. Marcus pulled away.

"Your woman gave us more of a fight than you," he said. "Ain't that right, Cego?"

The man with the patch chuckled again, the depth of his tone grating like nails on a chalkboard. "As much as she could fight," he snarled. "She screamed a lot. The young 'uns too."

Marcus gritted his teeth. He tightened his hands into fists, scraping his knuckles raw on the concrete, but said nothing to the men as they taunted him, poked at him, pleaded for him to accept the cold embrace of impending death. Instead he focused on their faces, memorizing every crease, every pore, every imperfection. He imprinted the sounds of their voices, inhaled their musty odors.

The red-bearded man raked at his chin with his fingers. "He's a goner," he said in a scratchy voice that barely sounded human. "Should we finish him?"

"Nah," said Cego. "I wanna watch him die slowly. Ain't often we get to watch."

"We don't have the time," said the Southerner with the scar. "I've got business elsewhere. We need to get what we can and hit the road. It's a long ride."

Cego sulked. "You're no fun, Rasgado."

Rasgado pressed his gloved hands against his knees and pushed himself to his feet. He stepped back from Marcus and walked toward the large wall-mounted cabinet that held the few weapons Marcus had kept since beating back the Cartel and escaping the reach of the Dwellers.

"I'll finish with the supplies," he said. "You two fill up your sacks and head back to the horses."

Marcus sank onto his heels. He could hear the men talking as they scavenged through his belongings, but couldn't discern what they were saying. The room was spinning like a clock whose second hand kept hitching as it moved around the face. He fell back and caught himself on the wall of the barn next to the door. His body shivered, his vision narrowed, his breathing was shallow and ragged.

Marcus closed his eyes, focusing on the stinging wounds that ravaged his body. He bit down on the inside of his cheek until the warm, coppery taste of his own blood filled his mouth.

After what seemed like hours, but likely was only minutes, the malodorous breeze of men brushing past him forced Marcus's eyes open. The red-bearded man stopped, the burlap sack dragging behind him, and smiled at him.

Marcus swallowed hard, motioning with his head for the man to come closer. The stranger obliged.

"What?" he asked in his scratchy voice. "You got a last word or something?"

Marcus whispered, "Name."

The intruder arched one of his thick bushy eyebrows. "My name?" he asked. "You want to know the name of the man who killed you?"

Marcus didn't answer. He widened his eyes as much as he could and stared at the man, tears leaking down his cheeks.

The man raked his beard. "Barbas."

Marcus weakly lifted his left hand and pointed at him, wagging his finger. "Kill," he muttered, "Barbas."

A yellow-stained smile snaked across the man's face. He patted Marcus on the top of his head with thick, calloused fingers. "Cute," he said. "You think you got life left in you."

The red-bearded Barbas planted his palm on the side of Marcus's face and shoved, pushing Marcus onto the floor. Then he kicked him in the back at the base of his spine and left through the open door.

Marcus coughed and groaned. He tried to keep his eyes open. He tried to breathe. In and out. In and out. But he was losing the fight.

Images of Lola, Sawyer, and Penny flashed in his mind. Wesson and Sylvia were there too. All of them stood together, beckoning him to join them. They were calling him by name. And for a moment, he was ready to join them. For a moment. Then it passed. Instead of warmth and light and joy, Marcus's wounded, bullet-riddled soul was filled with something else: the intensifying, primal need for revenge.

Chapter 2

OCTOBER 20, 2042, 5:32 PM
SCOURGE +10 YEARS
EAST OF RISING STAR, TEXAS

Marcus sat in the treehouse, absently running his hand along the smoothly hewn window ledge he'd hand sanded more than a decade earlier. He looked out across his land toward the highway.

The sun was low, passing in and out of thick puffy clouds that loped across a clear blue West Texas sky. A constant breeze ran its fingers across the tops of the tall grass between the road and the treehouse. The grass, undulating in waves, was losing its deep green in favor of something less vibrant.

Marcus took as deep a breath as he'd been able to suck down in three weeks and sighed. Something in the back of his mind had always warned him that his happiness was temporary, that the blessings of Lola, Sawyer, and Penny were bait, meant to lure him toward the surface before yanking him back into the depths of loneliness in which he'd lived for half of his life post-Scourge.

The apocalypse, as it were, wasn't about two-thirds of the world's population succumbing to an incurable pneumonia. It wasn't about the depraved Cartel with its insatiable thirst for violence and power, or the Dwellers who sought to supplant the Cartel with a hopefully less dystopian Texas. For Marcus, it was about pain. The pain of failing his family, of forgetting his training and allowing lesser men to best him, of aging ungracefully in a world that little valued what he might have had to offer it.

His eyes drifted across the land he'd called home for so long now; the pale green scrub, the mature oaks he'd planted himself which now struggled to survive against the drought, the orange kiss of the sun against the golden plain beyond his property and low undulating outline of the distant hills. They made this place familiar. They were the only things now.

Lola and the children had offered him the chance to redeem himself. To protect, to love, to teach. Somehow they'd managed to rebuild a semblance of normalcy in their hidden Eden. Lola was a good soul who had never sought to supplant Marcus's dead wife, Sylvia. Instead, she'd embraced the life Marcus had lived pre-Scourge, and encouraged him to talk about his memories, good and bad. She'd wanted him to understand that it was okay to be happy.

Sawyer, Lola's son, had been a solid young man. He'd been strong and a faithful hunting companion. He was wise beyond his years and Marcus had come to love him as he had his own son, Wes.

Little Penny had just turned six, they thought, although there'd been no way to know for sure. Her mother, Ana, had died so unexpectedly, they'd never had the chance to learn much about the baby they'd essentially adopted. Marcus thought Penny looked just like her mom, at least what he remembered of her, but she'd become a miniature Lola. If she wasn't asleep, Penny had followed Lola around at her hip. Her gestures, her inflection, her expressions all mimicked the woman she'd called Momma.

Marcus tapped the sill and curled his fingers to look at his nails. They were stuffed with dirt from the backyard. He picked at them, thinking about the morbid task that had packed the dirt as an awful reminder.

The breeze gusted and swirled through the open treehouse.

Marcus shivered and pulled up the collar on his ragged denim coat. He slid to the trapdoor and gingerly climbed down the planks of wood he'd hammered to the oak's sturdy trunk. He skipped the last rung and landed on the ground with a thud. The remnants of a dark stain on the blades of grass where he'd found Sawyer waved at him.

For three weeks Marcus had spent every waking moment doing one of three things. He'd worked to heal his wounds, he'd mourned the loss of his family, and he fixated on the memory of the faces of the three men who'd forced him to spend time on the other two tasks.

There was the man with the red beard, Barbas. His eyes were black and his beard long and stringy. The wiry tendrils stretched from his chin like a flame. His voice was coarse.

Rasgado was the man with the scar decorating the length of his angular face. His Southern drawl carried with it the barb of an uneducated man who thought he knew more than he did. His breath smelled like sour milk.

The stranger with the eye patch was called Cego. He'd somehow managed to stay fat in a place where most starved. His deep growl was unmistakable.

Marcus dealt the faces in his mind like a deck of cards, shuffling one after the other. He had no idea who they were or why they'd come. He suspected they weren't the work of the Dwellers. Otherwise they'd have told him that. There had been plenty of time for them to tell him while he lay dying.

They'd mocked him and robbed him and killed his family without cause. It didn't matter to Marcus who they were or their reason, if there was one, for ruining him. Marcus trudged back toward the barn, limping on his left leg, thanking them for giving him a reason to live and a life with nothing to lose.

As the sun dipped beneath the horizon and the last of its light glowed orange to the west, Marcus swung open the barn door and crossed the floor to one of the drop-in storage freezers. He pulled up the lid and braced it with a short two-by-four. Digging into the bottom of the empty icebox, he wiped a layer of frost from one of the corners and revealed a white pull tab. He tugged on the tab and yanked free a false bottom, which he tossed to the side.

Marcus balanced his weight on the edge of the freezer and reached deep to retrieve a large white pvc tube with caps on both ends. He heaved it from the freezer and leaned it against the side while he dove back into the icebox to pull out a second, smaller tube.

Holding one tube in each hand, Marcus shuffled across the floor to the workbench he used to prep, clean, and load his weapons. He laid the tubes on the table and began unscrewing the caps. As he slanted the tubes at an angle the contents slid free. They included a dozen packages of desiccant to absorb any moisture that may have remained inside the tubes when sealing with the end caps.

On the left side of the table was a large box of .30-06 ammunition. There were five hundred Berdan-primed steel-cased rounds in the box. Each one of them was like gold, a buried treasure Marcus had saved when all else failed.

To the right of the box was a Springfield M1903 rifle in an A4 sniper configuration. It was the same type of weapon Ernest Hemingway had carried in Africa. Marcus had bought it at a gun show two years before the Scourge. It was remarkably accurate and good for large game.

Sure, it didn't have the rapid-fire capability of an AR or any semiautomatic rifle, but it was all he had left. It would do.

The barrel and bolt were coated in grease, in addition to the desiccant, as an extra precaution. The rifle was prone to rusting otherwise, especially in a damp environment like a freezer.

He patted the rifle, ran his fingers along its polished wood stock, and slid open a drawer underneath the table. He fished around in the mess and found a tube of gun solvent.

Marcus slid the safety to the up position and the magazine selector to its center and slid out the bolt. Holding its weight in his hands, he twisted the back of the bolt and spun out the firing pin. It needed a fresh cleaning. Marcus tended to the weapon and reassembled it with ease.

He opened the box of ammo and plucked a silver Mauser clip from the top. The clip held five of the large .30-06 rounds and enabled easy loading. He loaded the clip, dropped the cartridges into the weapon, slid the bolt closed, and flipped the safety into the "safe" position. To the left of the bolt, he thumbed the magazine cutoff selector to the "on" position, which would allow him to quickly unload the five rounds like a traditional rifle.

The weapon had what Marcus liked to call "buttery smooth action". The bolt moved almost flawlessly, especially for a weapon designed more than a century earlier. It was accurate up to six hundred yards, maybe a little farther depending on the skill of the person firing the weapon. While it wasn't modern or sophisticated, the Springfield M1903A4 was a beautiful killing machine. Atop the Springfield was a fantastic scope. It was a Trijicon Variable Combat Optical Gunsight, whose optics could match the distance from which he was firing. At a close distance, he could use the scope without any magnification at all.

Marcus left the weapon on the table and moved across the room, passing the twin cots that, for five years, had served as beds for Sawyer and Penny. He tried not to look at them. They were both unmade, as they'd been on that deadly morning three weeks earlier. He'd found Penny still tucked underneath the hand-knotted quilt Lola had made from old salvaged sweatshirts. He'd known before he'd tried to pick her up there was no use.

Marcus brushed past the cots to one end of the large floor-to-ceiling storage rack he'd installed before the Scourge. It was more empty than full now, virtually devoid of food and bathroom comforts like two-ply toilet paper or quilted paper towels.

All that was left were boxes of baking soda, jugs of white vinegar, tools, empty plastic water bottles, some remnant first aid supplies.

The only thing edible on the shelves were two remaining jars of raw honey.

Marcus snagged a large hiking pack from one of the shelves and unzipped it. He stuffed it with the first aid kits, a couple of the water bottles, a plastic baggie with activated carbon granules he'd been saving since the Scourge, a plastic-cased automotive tool kit, and both jars of honey. He plucked a few sheets of workshop paper towels from a box and stuffed them into the bag.

Sidestepping along the shelving, he found a large mason jar and filled it with vinegar. At the opposite end of the barn closest to the freezer and the cots on which he and Lola slept were some folded clothes. It was mostly T-shirts, jeans, and some undergarments they'd scavenged and washed clean. He stuffed what he could into the pack and then zipped it closed.

His last stop was in the middle of the rack on the center shelf. He'd saved one last can of Zippo lighter fluid, a package of waterproof camping matches, and a flint spark torch igniter. They were next to a sleeping bag he wouldn't take and a four-person tent that comfortably slept two. He reached for the fluid and the matches and, while he was at it, took a foldable camping pot. He jammed the pot into the pack, slung the pack over both shoulders, walked back to get his weapons, and left the barn for the last time. He shivered as he stepped outside and he pulled his denim collar up around his neck. The clouds had blown past Rising Star, Texas, taking with them the blanket of warmth they'd provide through the night. Nearing midnight, a quarter moon hung halfway up the black sky. Marcus inhaled the chill and shrugged the pack onto his back.

He trudged through the crispy, knee-high grass to the garden, his boots crunching on the hardened soil. He sniffed past the chill and rubbed the cold from the tip of his nose, stepping across the rounded wood planks that framed the raised garden bed and into the softer, damp soil that coated the fruitful plot.

The carrots and celery were ready for harvest, as was some of the spinach. He picked a half-dozen carrots and dropped them into the vinegar-filled mason jar. The celery and spinach he wrapped in one of the shop towels and tucked into the outside backpack pocket.

Marcus wiped his hands on his pants and limped over to the small cemetery, which had more than doubled in size. There were five graves there now, all of them belonging to people Marcus had loved and whom he'd ultimately failed. He considered kneeling and praying. He thought about rekindling the conversations he'd long stopped having with Sylvia and Wesson.

Lola had freed him of his hallucinogenic discussions with dead people and his need to personify his weapons. She'd taught him life belonged to the living and was only worth having if one looked forward instead of back. She'd been right and he'd liked not being tied to the past, to his misdeeds and shortcomings. He'd relished the hope and expectations that came with wondering what beauty, however relative, the future might hold.

It would be easy for Marcus to forget what Lola had done for him and to slip back into the darkness of self-pity and mental flagellation. He didn't. He said a quiet goodbye to the women and children and walked from the cemetery without turning back.

The sun was low in the sky now, preparing to sink beneath the western horizon. He'd taken longer than planned to ready for his journey. Now was the time.

Marcus trudged to the far side of the barn, limping from the bullet wound that had slugged his thigh but had missed nerves, blood vessels, and bone. The injury, which he'd cleaned almost obsessively to prevent infection, was healing. But the muscle was damaged and it would be a while before the wound didn't moderately limit his endurance or speed.

He reached the northwestern corner of the barn, where the natural gas generator was closest to the well access he'd negotiated with the company that drilled his property. It had been a lifesaver in more ways than one. What had seemed like a foolhardy payment for the riches under his land had been a post-Scourge boon.

Marcus leaned his Springfield against the side of the building, picked up a pipe wrench, and applied it to the hookup that connected the generator to the barn. He turned the bright yellow valve perpendicular to the pipe and shut off the flow of gas. Then he cranked the wrench counterclockwise as hard as he could to loosen the connection at the nipple.

Several hard turns and the fitting came undone. Marcus removed it, leaving an open-ended pipe facing the side of the building. Then he turned the yellow valve to restart the flow of natural gas from the generator. The strong, putrid odor of mercaptan billowed from the open pipe.

He slung the rifle onto his shoulder and took a couple of steps back. Marcus took a breath through his mouth, trying to avoid the intensifying stench.

Next to the generator, he had piled a tangled mess of dead branches, limbs, leaves, and the pulled weeds from the nearby garden. He'd been building the mound of debris for close to a week, dragging to it whatever he could carry or pull through the high grass.

He uncapped the black can of Zippo lighter fluid, turned it on its side, and squeezed. A steady stream of the odorless liquid dousing the kindling and the ground around it. Marcus aimed the can at the side of the barn, painting it with the last of the fluid.

He tossed the can into the pile, lit a match, and tossed it too. The kindling sparked and flickered before the flames grew, licking at the sky.

He backed away quickly and hurried toward the fence line on the western edge of his property as the smoke blackened and chugged higher into the sky. By the time he'd reached the highway and turned west, the barn was ablaze.

Five years earlier, when his house had burned, Marcus thought of it as an unrecoverable loss. This time, as what was left burned purposefully, Marcus saw it as a cleansing. The place he'd built for shelter and protection hadn't turned out to be much of either.

The undulating glow of the hungry flames caught his peripheral vision as he walked. The winter breeze carried the smoke and its sharp odor toward him, above his head, and across the highway. Marcus was a man without a family and without a home. He was unchained and unbridled. And more than anything, he was looking forward to what was coming, at what he would unleash on the unsuspecting men who were destined now to suffer his wrath.

Chapter 3

OCTOBER 21, 2042, 6:32 AM
SCOURGE +10 YEARS
EAST OF RISING STAR, TEXAS

Marcus couldn't remember the last time it had rained. The clouds had threatened it repeatedly, but not delivered so much as spittle in weeks.

The road was cracked and dry, in such disrepair he was almost thankful he was on foot. The potholes and uneven asphalt would be a danger to a horse. He reasoned it was a good thing the thugs had taken his with them when they'd left him for dead.

The sun was behind him as he trudged eastward along Highway 36. It was low on the wavy horizon, barely tempering the coldest part of the day. The bolt-action Springfield was slung over his shoulder, a large pack strapped to his back, and he carried a Glock in his right hand. It was the only thing they'd left him, and it had only eight rounds in the magazine. One of them was already chambered.

Marcus was fifteen miles from his house and about forty from his first destination. He didn't know much about the world he'd abandoned for a second time, but Abilene was as close to a city as he was going to find. He might as well start there.

He figured it was a twenty-hour walk with his limp. He'd go until dark, or until his legs protested, and then he'd camp for the night. If he cut north on 283 and came into town due west on Interstate 20, he'd pass by a small lake. He could get water there, assuming the drought hadn't sucked it dry, and finish his hike the next day.

The rising sun rose, warming the back of Marcus's neck and his ears. His hair was cropped short and matched the scruff on his cheeks, chin, and neck. He'd taken a razor to his head during his convalescence. It was one less thing about which to worry.

As he passed a low-slung building on his right, his muscles tensed. He didn't like the idea of walking alone through a valley of abandoned buildings. There were too many places for people to hide, too many spots for an ambush. His eyes scanned the empty lot to his right. He swallowed against the dryness in his throat, his index finger twitching alongside the Glock's trigger guard.

He'd reached the Dairy Queen on the corner of 36 and South Main when the stubble tingled on the back of his sun-kissed neck. There was someone watching him.

Marcus caught a glimpse of movement to his left behind the old police department building, which sat catty-corner to the DQ. It was quick and only flashed for an instant in his peripheral vision, but Marcus was sure someone, or something, was there.

For a few steps he pretended as though he hadn't seen it. He kept his gaze forward, his gait the same, as he trekked through the town. He'd moved past Avenue E, near the 7-Eleven, when he saw it again. He heard it too: feet shuttling across gravel.

He quickly moved off the road and crouched behind a rusting gas pump under a dilapidated metal awning. There were two remaining pumps. From between them, Marcus saw the storefront and the gravel alleys that ran along either side of it.

He swiftly slid the Glock into his holster and looped the rifle strap over his head, shrugged the backpack off his shoulders, and placed it on the ground in front of him. He lay down on his stomach, legs splayed for balance, and rested the rifle on the pack. Within seconds he had one eye to the scope and the Springfield ready to fire. The safety was in the fire position and the magazine cutoff selector was on.

He blinked back a drop of sweat that trailed from a sudden bloom on his forehead. Through the scope he could see the remnants of the convenience store. The windows and doors were gone, save one untouched pane of glass to the right. The food racks and gondola shelves were toppled over, the glass doors to the refrigerators that lined the back of the store open or unhinged. There were signs of animals' nests and droppings littering the space. Marcus panned the area, looking for any movement. He searched the spaces to either side of the single-story concrete structure.

Then he saw it.

Pressed against the wall, to the left side of the building, was a brown shoe. It nearly blended with the dirt and gravel, but a wisp of dust gave it away. Marcus adjusted the scope, let out a deep breath to settle himself and waited until the shoe moved. It was nearly imperceptible, but it moved. Somebody was there.

A smirk crawled onto Marcus's face, but disappeared as quickly. He was protected from the threat he could see but ridiculously exposed to anyone behind him. Instinctively he twisted his body and looked behind him toward the empty, weedy lot that stretched for most of the block. There was nothing behind him.

He exhaled again and spun back around toward the 7-Eleven, settling his eye close to the scope. He repositioned the weapon to his previous spot at the left corner of the building and aimed downward at the ground to spot the shoe. It was gone.

Marcus lifted his head from the rifle and scanned the building, cursing under his breath, and returned to the scope. The threat had moved.

He had two choices. He could stay in position and lay in wait for the threat to reemerge, or he could load up and keep moving. Neither option was appealing. He cursed himself again.

Before he could flip a coin in his mind and choose the lesser of two evils, he heard the unmistakable whine of scraping metal straight ahead. He snapped the rifle to his right and zeroed in on the store. He couldn't see anything behind the racks or moving amongst the debris, but he knew the threat was there.

Marcus exhaled and leaned up from the scope. "Hey!" he called. "I don't want to kill you, but I've got you in my sights. My finger is on the trigger."

His voice echoed in the cool morning air, reverberating off the valley of abandoned stores and houses. Marcus listened to the echoing of his own voice, anticipating a response from the threat.

"You'll have to come out eventually," Marcus said when there was no reply. "Might as well save us both some time and do it now."

He lowered his eye to the scope and scanned fluidly from right to left. He was ready to move back to the right when a young girl no older than fifteen peeked out from behind a rack. She was wearing a worn Houston Astros baseball cap sideways. Her long black hair was frayed at the ends and covered her shoulders like wiry tentacles. Her bright eyes were narrowed in defiance as she raised her hands above her head.

Marcus lifted his head, looking for others. "Who's with you?"

The girl stepped forward, awkwardly maneuvering around the debris in the store. With her hands above her head, she moved from the store to the parking lot, her brown canvas shoes crunching on broken glass.

Marcus tapped the trigger guard with his fingertip. The rifle rested on the pack, its business end aimed at the girl, training on her as she walked closer to Marcus. Her dark eyes were focused on the weapon, her face expressionless.

"Are you alone?" Marcus asked.

The girl lowered her hands, her arms loose at her sides. She wiggled her fingers as if playing a concerto on an invisible piano. She tilted her head from one side to the other, cracking her neck, without taking her nasty glare off Marcus.

If she hadn't seemed dangerous, Marcus might have laughed at the absurdity of the teenage pugilist ready for a fight. She was gangly, her body not having quite grown into her spindly legs and boat-sized feet. Her long fingers were agile as she fluttered them musically. Her thumbs curved outward, giving them an almost clawlike appearance. Marcus marveled at how the girl's tiny, dark features were impish, but her dead eyes gave away that she'd led anything but a carefree childhood.

He sighed, growing tired of the pubescent grandstanding. "You need to—"

Without warning, and with incredible quickness, the girl drew a knife from behind her back and flung it at Marcus's head. The sunlight glinted off the blade as it hurled toward him, but he didn't have time to react. It whipped past his head and nailed a wooden utility pole right behind him.

As he jerked his head away from the knife's path, he instinctively slid his finger to the trigger, ready to fire. But he didn't. He didn't want to kill the child. "Hey," he said sternly, as would a father scolding his disobedient child, "put your hands up now. Both of them over your head. Or I pull this trigger."

The girl pouted and raised her hands. She rested them on her ball cap and laced her fingers.

"Stay put," he ordered. "One stupid move and you're toast. Do you understand?"

The girl didn't acknowledge Marcus as he pushed himself to his feet and approached her with the rifle aimed at her chest. He was close enough to see the patch of faint acne populating her chin.

"Do you understand English?" he asked. *"¿Habla Español?"*

The girl shrugged.

"I don't want to hurt you," said Marcus. "Do you understand me? Can you understand what I'm saying?"

The girl inhaled and let out a sigh.

Marcus adjusted the rifle, tightening the stock's position against his shoulder. His gut told him to leave the feral child by herself and move on. He had places to be and people to kill. Still, there was something about her that had him transfixed. Maybe it was her guile, her aggression, her obvious will to survive.

He motioned to the right. "Turn around."

The girl hesitated.

Marcus jabbed the barrel toward her. "Now."

She turned around, her back to Marcus. Her shirt was torn across the top, as if she'd snagged it on something sharp. Protruding from her cinched waistband was the matte black steel handle of a throwing knife.

"I'm taking the knife," Marcus said. He held the rifle with his right hand and reached for the knife with his left. When his hand touched the handle, the girl quickly spun, grabbed his wrist, and twisted it.

Acting without thinking, Marcus backed up and pulled hard, yanking the girl off balance enough that he regained control of the knife and wrestled it free from her as she struggled to stay on her feet. He moved quickly away from her, the knife in one hand and the rifle in the other.

He checked over one shoulder and the other, keeping the girl in his line of sight. She was alone. If she hadn't been, companions would have shown themselves. Marcus tucked the knife into his waistband.

"You've got fight," he said. "That's good. It'll keep you alive."

The girl wiped her face with the back of her hand. Her chin was tilted toward her chest and she looked up at Marcus with demon eyes that glowed from behind the dark curtain of hair that hung in front of her face. She was breathing through her mouth, her jaw slack. Her chest heaved and her tattered shirt hung from her body. Her fingers were curled into fists. Marcus sighed and limped backward toward his pack. He kept the girl in front of him as he retreated in a defensive but ready posture. He'd wasted enough time here. She clearly didn't want his help and saw him as a threat. Without her knives, she was relatively harmless.

Still facing her, he crouched down, wincing at the pressure on his leg, and grabbed his pack. He slung it over one shoulder, not willing to risk putting down his rifle to put on the pack properly, and backed onto the road. He stopped at the utility pole and levered the knife free of the wood.

"You dropped your hat," he called, and turned to resume his march toward Abilene. He'd gone a half-dozen steps when she spoke.

"You can't take my knives," she called out to him. "I need them."

Marcus looked over his shoulder at the girl. The hat was in her hand and she ran her fingers across its curved brim. Suddenly the feral demon looked every bit the frightened child. Marcus adjusted the pack on his shoulder and waited for her to speak again.

"Can I please have my knives?"

"Why?" he asked. "I give you the knives and you'll kill with them."

Her features softened. "I promise I won't," she said. "I ain't got nobody, just me and my knives."

Marcus looked west, in the direction he was going, and then back east from where he'd come. The sun cast a hazy glow in what was now a pale blue sky. A bird flapped overhead and then glided toward a cluster of scrub oaks on the northern side of the highway. He clenched his jaw.

"We're in a no-win situation," he said to the girl. "I give you the knives, you wing one at me and stick me in the back as I walk away. I take the knives and you probably don't last a week out here."

The girl lifted the hat and set it on her head, spinning the brim to the side. She fingered her hair from her eyes, pulling it back across her shoulders, and shrugged.

"How long you been out here alone?" Marcus asked.

She eyed the ground in front of her feet and her lips moved as if she were trying to count the days. "A year or two," she said. "Could be longer. I stopped counting."

"What's your suggestion?" asked Marcus. "You're smart. What would you do if you were me?"

A smirk dimpled one of the girl's cheeks and she took a step closer to Marcus. "How about you leave the knives in the pole there. Jab 'em real good. I stay where I am, and when you're far enough away, I get my knives. You go your way and I go mine."

Marcus glanced at the utility pole and then back at the girl. "That doesn't help me out. You tried to kill me."

The girl's smirk evaporated. Her expression flattened and her eyes went cold. "There are bad people out there who need killing. Hard to tell them from the others sometimes."

Marcus worked to suppress a grin. She was years younger than him but maybe just as wise. After all, they'd both lived post-Scourge for the same amount of time and, as a percentage of her life, she'd lived it longer. He ran his fingers along the twin knife handles tucked at his waist.

"You're right about that," he said. "We don't know enough about each other to know whether either or both of us need killing, right?"

The girl cocked her head to one side like a confused puppy. Her brow furrowed.

"Let's figure it out," he said. "I can't leave you here to die if you're the kind that needs to live, but I can't give you your knives if I'm the kind that needs to live. So how about I keep the knives for now, you tag along with me, and I keep you fed? We get to know each other, and at some point we'll figure each other out."

The girl wiggled her fingers at her side. "And then I get my knives back?"

"Depends on what kind of person you are."

She huffed. "Or what kind *you* are."

"Exactly. I'm heading west to Abilene."

The girl adjusted the cap on her head, her eyes widening with uncertainty. "There are bad people in Abilene."

"There are bad people everywhere," said Marcus. Marcus shrugged the pack higher on his back and started walking away from the girl. His leg ached, but it wasn't unbearable. The stiffness from the morning chill was nearly gone. He'd walked a couple of dozen steps when he heard quick footsteps pattering against the asphalt.

The girl sidled up to Marcus and slowed her pace. "You said something about food," she said. "And water?"

Marcus unhooked the canteen from the side of his pack and handed it to the girl. She uncapped it and gulped, streams of water trickling down her cheeks.

"Not too fast," Marcus said. "You'll get sick."

The girl took another large gulp, storing it in her cheeks, and handed back the canteen. What was left of the water sloshed around the inside. Marcus drew it to his mouth and slugged a mouthful. He swished it around in his mouth and curled his cracked lips around his teeth, moistening them.

"We're gonna head north in a bit," he said. "We'll camp for the night. There's a lake south of I-20. We'll hit it by nightfall."

The girl bobbed her head and fingered her hair behind her ear, tucking it away from her face. Marcus slid the knives along his waistband to his right, away from the girl.

Chapter 4

OCTOBER 21, 2042, 12:53 PM
SCOURGE +10 YEARS
SOUTH OF BELLE PLAIN, TEXAS

Marcus heard the crack of a rifle and crouched. He unslung the Springfield from his shoulder, gripped it with both hands, and waved the girl behind him as he moved to the north side of Highway 36. At the edge of the road was a drainage ditch that separated the disintegrating asphalt shoulder from a high-tensile cattle fence.

Another crack thundered through the air and pushed Marcus to his chest in the dirt and dying weeds. The girl was at his left hip, mimicking his prone position.

"I can't see where it's coming from," he said. He lowered his eye to the scope and scanned the horizon, breathing in and out slowly, trying to regulate his thumping, rapid pulse.

The girl inched forward, pulling herself along the ditch on her elbows. She was three body lengths ahead of Marcus when she glanced back at him over her shoulder. "It's near the intersection up there," she said. "There are two people. They've both got guns, it looks like."

Marcus narrowed his eyes and checked the scope again. He zeroed in on the intersection with US 283, which was three or four hundred yards ahead. Tucked behind a pair of graying scrub oaks was a man with a rifle. He couldn't see the other person and lifted his eye from the scope. The girl had turned around and was inching her way back toward him.

"I only see one," he said. "How do you see two?"

"I'm not old like you," she said. "There's the one with the gun at the tree, and on the opposite corner, there's one hiding behind some bushes. They've got a horse too."

Marcus looked again through the scope. He panned to the right, adjusting his elbow, and picked out the second person at a cluster of dense yaupon. There was a horse there too. He'd missed it the first time.

A third crack rolled through the air and a round zipped past Marcus close enough for him to hear it. A fourth followed quickly and splintered a fence post a couple of feet from Marcus's head.

"Give me the knives," the girl said flatly.

Marcus shook his head. "Not gonna happen. I'll take them out."

"You fire once and the one you don't hit will know exactly where you are," she said. "He'll see the muzzle flash and you'll be dead. And that's assuming you hit the target with the first round. That rifle looks older than you."

Marcus checked the scope and then looked at the girl again. He could feel the knives pressed flat against his hip. "What are you going to do?"

"You take the one with the horse," she said. "I'll roll under the fence and surprise the other one. As soon as you fire, I'll throw. Or I could take your pistol."

Marcus smirked. "That's not happening."

The girl leaned forward on her elbows and shrugged. "Suit yourself. I'll just wait until you're dead and take my knives."

Marcus smiled and lowered his eye to the scope. He exhaled and focused on the man at the yaupon. "Sounds like a plan. Now get behind me."

While the girl moved, muttering under her breath, Marcus slid his finger along the trigger guard. He leveled the crosshair at the man's head, adjusted the scope for the four-hundred yard distance, and then swung quickly to the right to find the other shooter. He practiced the move twice as another shot buzzed above them.

He made sure the safety was off and the magazine cutoff was flipped to the on position. Marcus focused the center of the target on the man's chest and slid his finger to the Springfield's trigger. He exhaled, steadied his aim, and fired.

The rifle kicked into his shoulder and the blast echoed loudly through the air. Without waiting to see if the bullet hit the target, he quickly swung to the right, cycling the rifle's bolt. The round chambered automatically from the internal magazine and he set the crosshair on the second target's chest. The man was taking aim himself.

Marcus pulled the trigger at the moment the target's weapon flashed. The twin rifle shots cracked like simultaneous bolts of thunder and a round slugged the edge of the trench next to Marcus's left arm when the target spun and dropped his weapon, falling into the trunk as he collapsed.

Marcus swung his rifle back to the left and, through the scope, saw the man tangled at the edge of the yaupon, the thin branches suspending his limp body. His rifle was on the ground.

"You were saying?" Marcus said to the girl.

"That you're old. And you should have let me taken care of one of them."

"Did you not just see—"

"My dad used to say even a stopped clock is right twice a day," she said, pushing herself to her feet. "You got lucky, especially with that...what's the word? Musket."

Marcus rolled his eyes, set the safety, and using the rifle as a cane, eased himself from the ground. He adjusted the heavy pack against his back and cinched its waist strap. He slung the rifle over his shoulder, checked at his hips for his Glock and the girl's knives, and stepped up onto the asphalt. The edge of the shoulder crumbled under the weight of his boot.

He motioned toward the intersection. "Let's go see about these two, but don't go near the weapons. If you do, we've got a problem."

The girl huffed. "Fine."

Marcus limped purposefully toward the man at the yaupon. As he got closer, he could see the grisly wound on the man's chest. On the ground not far from the man's dangling fingertips was his weapon, a Remington 700. Marcus recognized the popular bolt-action rifle's stainless-steel bar barrel and its walnut stock with the distinctive black fore-end cap. It was a beautiful weapon.

He bent over and picked up the rifle, feeling its heft in his left hand. He rounded the corner, turning south onto 283 behind the yaupon, and approached the horse. It was a deep brown with white splotches across its hind end. Marcus moved slowly to the animal at its side. He slid the rifle into a saddle scabbard and ran his hand along its smooth coat. He checked a saddlebag and found a half-empty box of Remington .30-06 ammunition. He smiled at the good fortune and latched the bag closed.

"It's a bay blanket," said the girl. She was standing in the middle of the road, a good twenty feet from Marcus.

"What is?"

"The pattern on the horse," she said. "My dad used to have one. He had a bay blanket Appaloosa and a Grulla blanket. It was silvery and white."

Marcus patted the horse gently, admiring the loud-colored mare. "Good to know." He left the horse tied to the brittle, jagged stump of a dead mesquite and moved back to the dead man.

He was wearing dirt-stained cargo pants and a sweatshirt that rode up his hairy back, revealing his gray skin beneath the dark tendrils. Marcus grabbed the man's ankles and yanked him free of the yaupon tangle. He laid the man flat on the dirt at the shoulder of the highway, leaving a dark red streak on the ground where the dead man's head bopped along the gravelly earth. His sweatshirt rode up his back and caught at his pits. The wide swirls of dark hair painted the man's back like paisleys. Marcus dropped the feet when he noticed the backs of the man's hands. Barely visible beneath the hair on each hand was a black tattooed dollar sign. They were the same tattoos as the ones on the hands of the red-bearded man named Barbas.

Marcus gritted his teeth and balled his fists. He squeezed his hands as tight as he could and then kicked the dead man's side hard enough a rib snapped. He cursed loudly then looked over at the girl. "Sorry."

"I've heard worse," she said. "I've seen worse."

Marcus fished through the man's pockets, but they were empty. He crossed the road to the other man, the one who'd hidden behind the tree.

That man was a heap, his body awkwardly leaning against the trunk. His eyes were open, as was the hole between them that leaked a crooked creek of blood down his nose and around his open mouth. His tongue hung at the side, protruding between two rows of canary yellow teeth that looked like pieces of candy.

One hand was twisted behind his back, the other palm down on the ground. It too had the dollar-sign ink. Marcus cursed again.

"What is it?" asked the girl.

"I should have left one of them alive," said Marcus. "They know somebody I'm looking for."

"Who's that?"

He knelt down and picked the man's empty pockets, trying to breathe through his mouth. The man reeked of cheap moonshine but had nothing else to offer other than the AR-15 lying in the dirt.

Marcus picked up the Colt-made rifle and checked its magazine. It was empty. He pulled it tight against his shoulder, aimed it toward the open field beyond the cattle fence, and pulled the trigger. The weapon kicked and blasted the last round from the barrel.

He walked over to the girl. "Here, you can have this one."

The girl narrowed her eyes with suspicion but took the gift and held it in her hands. She put one hand around the pistol grip and, with the other, wrapped her fingers around the vented handguard. She aimed it at the ground in front of Marcus's feet.

"I'm guessing it's empty," she said, one eyebrow arched higher than the other.

"Yep."

"Then what's the point?"

"I can't carry three rifles," said Marcus, "and I'm not letting you have a loaded one. At least you *look* dangerous."

The girl rolled her eyes. "Great. What now?"

"We ride the horse to our camping spot."

Marcus undid the clove hitch on the rope tying the horse to the dead mesquite, helped the girl struggle into the saddle, and climbed on behind her.

"Hold on to the saddle horn," he said, kicking the horse forward with his heels.

The Appaloosa snorted and moved onto the highway heading due north, its shoes clacking on the asphalt in a four-beat gait. Marcus let the mare go at her pace, not pushing her to go faster than she intended. He held the reins on either side of the girl.

"Who is it you're trying to find?" she asked again.

The horse walked north, fighting against a wind that blew from the west. A thin layer of clouds drifted across the sun, casting a mosaic of shadows across the road ahead.

Marcus took a deep breath and exhaled. "Somebody who needs killing."

Chapter 5

OCTOBER 21, 2042, 8:53 PM
SCOURGE +10 YEARS
SOUTH OF BAIRD LAKE, TEXAS

The fire crackled and popped, embers dancing through the smoke and climbing into the night toward the black sky. The clouds had long since moved on, leaving the stars to shine and strobe as they always had above West Texas. Marcus loved the stars. He often considered the light from those stars as a window to the past, a time before the Scourge. When the light from those ancient stars millions of light years away had begun traveling through space, Earth was a much different place.

As it traveled through space on its way toward his evolving planet, dinosaurs ruled on the ground and in the sky. Then man came and he ruled, an unstoppable force, until a viral pneumonia killed two-thirds of the population.

At some point on the light's journey, Marcus was born and fell in love. He married and fought in war. He came home and became a father. He worked to protect his family and lost everything.

Marcus settled against his pack, which he'd leaned against a watermelon-sized rock, and folded his arms against his chest. The heat from the fire lapped at his face in waves, providing intermittent breaks from the night chill.

The girl sat across from him on the opposite side of the flames. She was tearing off pieces of lettuce and shoving them into her mouth. She chewed with her mouth wide open, chomping on the earthy greens. Her face glowed orange from the fire, but her eyes were still so black they killed the light that hit them. Marcus was convinced she hid evil in those eyes—either hers or someone else's.

"What's your name?" Marcus asked over the crackling flames.

"What's yours?" the girl countered, a piece of lettuce flying from her mouth.

"Marcus Battle."

"Battle?" asked the girl. "Like war?"

"Yeah."

The girl swallowed another mouthful of lettuce. "That's a stupid name. It's like a comic book character or from one of those lame stories my dad used to read on his iPad."

Marcus ignored the insult. "You know what an iPad was? And comic books?"

"Sure," she said. "I'm not stupid."

"I didn't say that," Marcus said. "You're just young, that's all. What are you? Fifteen?"

The girl ripped another strip of lettuce and stuffed it in her mouth. "Seventeen. I was in first grade."

"When the Scourge happened?"

"Yep."

Marcus reached for the canteen hooked to the side of his pack. "So what's your name?"

"Lou."

"Lou?"

"Lou."

"That's a boy's name."

"It's short for Louise," she said. "I don't like Louise."

Marcus took a swig of water and wiped his face with the back of his hand. He capped the jug and leaned forward, reaching out and around the flames. She took the offering and guzzled the water. Her gulps sounded like a toddler downing a sippy cup of apple juice.

"Lou it is, then," he said. "You can call me Marcus."

Lou came up for air, breathing heavily. "I'm sure as heck not calling you Battle."

"Was Lou your dad's name too?"

The girl's hardened features softened. Her shoulders slumped and she wiped her nose with the collar of her T-shirt.

"I called him Dad."

A breeze filtered through their campsite, blowing the smoke and embers toward Marcus. He squeezed his eyes against the acrid burn and coughed. The breeze shifted and cleared the air. He knuckled the corners of his eyes. "Can I ask what happened to him?"

Lou stiffened. "You can ask."

Marcus smirked and stood from his seat. "I need to get water. Why don't you come with me?"

"I'm good," said Lou.

"I'm not asking." Marcus motioned toward the lake with his head, pulled a plastic bottle from his bag, and Lou grumbled her way from the ground to his side.

They were camped on the eastern edge of an oval dirt road that looped along the southwestern side of Baird Lake. In the middle of the oval was a grassy field littered with abandoned mobile homes and trailers. There were eight of them. There were also two empty single-story houses. Marcus had checked them when they'd arrived.

Extending from the eastern edge of the dirt road to the lake was a trio of worn, weedy paths that had likely served as boat ramps at one time. Marcus and Lou walked toward the water. The only light was the waxing quarter moon and its reflection on the water. It was enough, though, to guide them to the lake's edge.

Marcus dipped the bottle into the water and felt it glug until it was full. He handed it to Lou and told her to carry it back to the camp.

She begrudgingly agreed and they moved back along the path to the fire.

The lake had, at one time, been surrounded by oil fields and later towering wind turbines that harnessed the raw power of the Texas winds. Now the place was a virtually deserted dust bowl where those same winds carried the soil aloft and coated the lake with its minerals. The lake was fed by a natural spring, Baird Springs, which, at the time Scourge began was the only remaining active springs in Callahan County. Marcus made a mental note to someday locate the springs just to see if it was still flowing. That is, if he survived what lay ahead in his quest to find the tattooed men who killed his family and left him to die.

Returning to the campfire, Lou held up the bottle against the flames and turned it in her hand. "This is gross," she said of the opaque brownish liquid filling the plastic container. "I can't drink this."

"Hold your horses," said Marcus. "It'll be fine."

He reached into his pack and pulled out a second large plastic bottle. He set it next to the pack and then removed his first aid kit, the automotive tool kit, and a couple of paper towels. From the first aid kit, he took a straight needle. From the tool kit, he grabbed a pair of pliers.

He grasped the needle with the pliers and held it at the base of the fire, rolling it over as it heated up; then he used the hot needle to poke several holes in the bottom of the empty plastic bottle.

"What are you doing?" asked Lou.

"You'll see," said Marcus. He eased back next to his pack and pulled out a baggie filled with activated carbon. Carefully, he poured a quarter of the contents into the bottle.

"What's that stuff?"

"Activated carbon."

"Activated carbon?" asked Lou. "Something everyone just has lying around ten years after a plague."

"I used to hunt with my kid," said Marcus. "I had stashes of this stuff for this very reason. You never know when you're going to need clean water."

Marcus took a paper towel and rolled it into a tight cone, folding over the end of the paper towel to close the hole and stuffing it into the dry, carbon-filled bottle. He unhooked the canteen from the side of his pack, withdrew a folded camping pot, and then moved around the fire to sit next to Lou. He placed the pot on the ground in front of her and set the carbon bottle in the middle of it.

"Go ahead," he said. "Pour the water into the bottle."

Lou eyed him for a moment but followed instructions. Slowly, she emptied the dirty lake water into the bottle, clean water draining through the holes in the bottom of the bottle and into the pot. Once the long process was finished, Marcus drained the pot into the canteen. Then he set the closed canteen at the edge of the fire.

"Got to let it boil a bit," he said. "Then it's good to go."

"We can drink it?"

"Yep."

Lou was staring blankly into the fire. "Huh." She blinked and looked over at Marcus. "My dad used to say there are two types of people. Those who are smart and those who think they are."

Marcus moved to his bag and repacked his belongings. The two sat quietly for a few minutes, staring at the flames lapping at the embers, as if trying to catch them before they floated skyward.

Finally, Marcus cleared his throat. "I'll bite. Which am I?"

Lou took her hat off, set it on the ground beside her, and scratched her head with both hands. "You're either one or the other."

Marcus zipped the pack closed and chuckled. "And you?"

"I'm both."

"Of course you are," Marcus said, standing. He tugged at the collar of his shirt and scratched at the healing wound in the area between his neck and shoulder.

"What happened there?" asked Lola.

Marcus touched the tender skin with his fingers. "I got shot."

"And you didn't die?"

"I'm assuming that's a rhetorical question given that I'm alive and we're having a conversation."

Lou pursed her lips.

"No." He sighed. "I didn't die. The bullet went straight through. There was a lot of blood though. Kinda thought I'd been hit in the chest. So did the men who did it."

Lou's eyes widened with an epiphany. "And that's who we're—"

"Both of us need to get some sleep," Marcus cut in. "We're heading out early. We've got a marathon tomorrow. The horse will help, but I want to make Abilene long before sundown."

He picked up the camping pot and scraped it along the ground, shoveling loose dirt and shallow weeds into it. Then he dumped it onto the fire, weakening the flames. Another two pot loads had it out within minutes.

Marcus checked to make sure he had the two rifles, the Glock, and the knives secured beneath the pack and then laid his head on the bag. He looked up at the stars and listened to the wind whip around the camp. He raised the collar on his denim jacket and folded his arms across his chest to tuck his hands under his pits. It was getting colder without the fire's ambient heat.

"My dad told me the story about Marathon," Lou said softly. "It was a battle between the Greeks and the Persians."

Marcus closed his eyes and listened. He inhaled the fading scent of burning wood and smoke.

"Philippides, a messenger, was sent to Sparta to ask for help when the Persians landed in Marathon," Lou continued. "When the Greeks won, he ran from the battlefield in Marathon to Athens to deliver the news. He ran so far and so hard that right after he told everybody about the victory, he died."

"It's a fable, you know," said Marcus.

"The run or the death?"

"Both."

"Does it matter?"

"What?"

"That it's not real?" she asked, a snip in her tone. "It's a good story. It's about a man who gave his life for something bigger. That's a good story."

"Maybe," Marcus conceded.

Lou was quiet for a moment; then she chuckled. "I've decided."

Marcus sighed. "What?"

"You're the kind who *thinks* he's smart."

CHAPTER 6

OCTOBER 22, 2042, 2:53 PM
SCOURGE +10 YEARS
ABILENE, TEXAS

Abilene wasn't Abilene anymore. At least it wasn't the post-Scourge Cartel-run city Marcus remembered the last time he'd moseyed through its wide streets and fire-bombed Bible Hardware. But it wasn't the city in which he'd spent so much time in the years before the end of the world as he knew it.

The drought had painted the city in dust and grime. The constant wind whipped it into Marcus's eyes and into his nose. He reached for the half-empty canteen. He'd given most of the water to Lou and the Appaloosa, figuring they needed it more than him. Now his cracked lips burned and a headache was knocking at the back of his head.

He uncapped the canteen and took a long pull from it. He let the warm water sit in his mouth, soaking into his dry tongue, relishing it washing down his throat.

They clopped along east Highway 80, which forked westward as Interstate 20 raced north around the city. The distantly familiar orange and white striped A-frame roof of a Whataburger reminded Marcus they were only a couple of blocks from the center of town.

Unlike the smaller enclaves through which he'd traveled, Abilene still resembled civilization, as rough as it might be. There were people nervously milling about at the edges of the wide streets. Men and women hurried about, hand in hand, their heads down. Although there was a palpable anxiety that hung low over the streets, there were signs of life. Marcus slowed the horse to a stop and hopped to the street, offering up a hand to help Lou down.

He looked up to the sky, past the increasingly dense rows of buildings on either side of the wide street. A pair of blackbirds circled high above, gliding on the chilly breeze that whistled through what might have passed as the town's commercial center.

Marcus tied the horse to an old newspaper vending machine bolted to the sidewalk above the high concrete curb that ran the length of the boulevard. The coin-operated box was a dusty brown and the blue star in the *Reporter-News* masthead logo was faded. The racks in the machine itself were empty.

Up ahead to the right was the charred exterior of the former home of Bible Hardware. Marcus had shopped at the family-run business for years before the Scourge. He'd also blown it up five years earlier when it served as a local headquarters for the Cartel, a network of criminals who'd put most of Texas under their bloodstained thumb.

Marcus withdrew the Remington from the scabbard, patted the horse, and walked to the middle of the street and westward a few steps to get a better look at the black streaks that fanned outward from the shattered glass entrance. He held the rifle, balancing its weight in his open right hand as he stared at the building.

Lou joined Marcus at the road's center. "Somebody must have been angry to set fire to a place like that," she said. "It looks like it got bombed."

"It did," Marcus said. "Actually it was grenades."

Lou moved around to face Marcus with a furrowed brow. "How do you know?"

"Because I did it."

A smile spread across her face. "I'm impressed. I've been past that place I don't know how many times and I always wondered what happened."

Marcus started moving again. "C'mon, I need your help."

"Why?" Lou asked. "With what?"

"You said you'd been here," said Marcus. "You said there were bad people here. I need you to show me where they hang out, where they live."

Marcus wiped his sweating forehead with the back of his left hand and pulled the rifle up to cradle it diagonally across his chest. Lou kept pace, her footsteps dragging along the asphalt twice as fast as Marcus's longer, slower stride.

"I'll need my knives," she said. "I'm not kidding."

Marcus kept walking, scanning both sides of the street. A woman peeked her head through an open window on the second floor of a three-story brick building. She leaned on the sill with her elbows locked and her palms flat against the wood. Marcus nodded at her. The woman didn't respond.

"Marcus," Lou persisted, "you need to give me my knives."

Marcus ran his tongue along the back of his teeth and whistled. It was the first tune that popped into his head, one about which he'd not thought in a long time. He remembered the melody, though, as if he'd heard it on the radio only minutes before.

"You're ignoring me," said Lou, shrugging the rifle strap on her shoulder. "Stop ignoring me. And stop whistling."

Marcus whistled more loudly, bobbing his head. He smiled at Lou with his eyes, raising his eyebrows in a dramatic, sarcastic arch.

"What are you whistling?" she asked. "What song is that?"

Marcus licked his lips. "Do you know where we're headed? You know where people get together here?"

Lou nodded and pointed her finger down the street. "A few blocks from here," she said. "What's the tune?"

"It's called 'Don't Worry, Be Happy,'" he said and started whistling again.

Lou huffed. "That's stupid," she said loudly enough for Marcus to hear her above his tootle, "and I'm not going any further until you give me the knives."

"You have your rifle."

"I don't have any bullets," she whined. "Plus I'm not good with a gun. I'm good with knives."

"It's farther, by the way," he said.

"What?"

"You said further. It's farther. Whenever you're describing a measurable distance, it's farth—"

"Give me my knives, Marcus."

"Let's see what happens first," said Marcus. "Not everybody is a bad guy. We might be able to get some good information without having to engage in violence."

Lou rolled her eyes. "I'm not going."

Marcus shrugged and started walking again. "Suit yourself," he said over his shoulder. "I die in there, you're never getting your knives back."

He resumed whistling and pushed ahead. A half mile later he heard a commotion coming from a single-story steel building with an open hangar door. There were a couple of large men standing on either side of the door. Beyond the opening, there was what looked like a bar. Next to the building was a large rumbling generator. There were several power cords running from it into the bar. It appeared to be the kind of generator would-be preppers might have in their garages ahead of hurricane season. It was enough to keep ice cold and fans running. Marcus hadn't seen one in years. He didn't know anybody even had fuel enough to run them anymore.

Still whistling, Marcus opened the bolt on the Remington and approached the would-be bouncers with his left hand in the air above his head. The thicker of the two men stepped forward, a frown painted on his face.

"I don't recognize you," said the man. "Who are you?"

Marcus smiled. "Marcus Battle. I've been walking for hours on my way west. Just need a little something to make the traveling more tolerable."

The bouncer eyed Marcus up and down and grunted. "Where'd you come from?"

"East of Rising Star," he said. "Camped out overnight." He unhooked the canteen with one hand and shook it to show it was empty.

"Give me the knives you got and you can go in," the man said.

Marcus glanced at the handles protruding from his waist then over his shoulder. He didn't see Lou. "To borrow?"

"To keep," he said. "Consider it your cover charge. And you best keep those bolts open on the rifles."

"Sure thing."

"I'm gonna need that Glock too," said the other bouncer. "You can't go inside with it."

Marcus looked through the opening into the bar. There were several men with guns on their hips or on the tables in front of them. He motioned toward them with his chin. "What about them?" he asked. "All of them have their guns."

"We know them," said the first guard. "We don't know you."

"You got any more in that pack?" asked the second.

"No," said Marcus. "You can check."

The guards looked at each other; then the first said, "Nah. Give us the knives and the Glock and you're good."

Marcus reluctantly obliged and stepped into the bar. It took a moment for his eyes to adjust to the dimmer light. When they did, he found the bar off to the left and weaved his way amongst the handful of crowded tables.

The barkeep dropped a glass in front of him as he approached the worn oak bar. He was an older man, gaunt, with eyes that sank deep into his narrow face. His mouth was puckered from lack of teeth and his shirt hung on him as if it were sized for a man twice as big.

"What do you want?" he asked, his voice raspy and weak.

Marcus leaned on the bar, conscious of the eyes drilling holes in his back. Everyone in the bar, he was sure, was watching him. "What do you have?"

"Handcrafted spirits."

"I'll take that."

The man poured the light brown liquid from a large mason jar, stopping when he'd emptied the equivalent of two shots into the glass. He wiped the edge of the jar with a crusty towel and then slapped the rag over his shoulder.

"How you plan to pay?" the man croaked.

"What do you take?" asked Marcus.

"Food, depending on what it is; ammo, depending on what it is; pretty much anything, depending on—"

Marcus raised his glass and winked. "What it is," he said, finishing the barkeep's sentence.

The man smacked his lips at the interruption and grumbled, muttering under his breath. He set the mason jar on the counter. "What do you got?"

"Thirty ought six? I can give you a few rounds."

The man scratched his weak chin. "All right," he said. "Five rounds a shot. You got two shots there. So give me ten."

"Three rounds a shot," Marcus countered. "Five for the two."

The man smirked. "Six for the two."

"Okay," said Marcus. "Six it is."

He laid both rifles on the bar and slid the pack from his shoulders. He reached into the bag and pulled out a handful of rounds. He counted six and slid them to the keep.

"Much obliged," said the man, fingering the ammunition and dropping them into his T-shirt breast pocket.

Marcus zipped up the pack and dropped it gently onto the floor at his feet. He picked up the glass, took a courtesy sip of the bitterly strong mash, and forced a smile at the keep. Then he spun around and leaned on the bar with his back, putting his weight on his uninjured leg.

As he surveyed the motley crowd, he half expected to see loose women in hoop skirts and an ace-high piano player with sleeve garters on his arms. He took another hesitant sip as a crooked-nosed man walked up to him at the bar.

"You're new," he said, his drawl turning one-syllable words into two. "I seen you walk in."

"Yep," said Marcus. "I'm new."

The tip of the man's nose moved up and down as he spoke. "You're looking for somebody."

"Is it that obvious?"

"To everybody but a blind man," said the man, planting his palms on the bar next to Marcus. "Nice rifles. That a Springfield?"

Marcus nodded. "Sniper configuration."

"So you ain't lookin' for friends, then?"

Marcus took another sip, winced, and swallowed it.

The man leaned closer to Marcus. "I bet I can help you find your somebody," he said under his breath. "I know lots of somebodies."

"Tell me this," Marcus said. "How many of these folks are Dwellers?"

The man leaned back, his eyes wide with surprise. "Dwellers?" He chuckled. "Where you been, fella? Ain't nobody Dwellers no more. At least not here. Them people was in control for a hot minute."

Marcus put down his drink. "What do you mean?"

"I mean we might have been better off under the Cartel," he said. "At least they kept order and such. When they split and the Dwellers came in, it was…it was like…hey, you know about Syria?"

"What about it?"

The man wagged his finger excitedly, but kept his voice low. "Before the Scourge, before the Cartel, you remember that war in

Syria? The one that led to the camps that led to the disease and such?"

"Yeah."

"Well, it's like that now," said the man. "After we went into Syria and left, there was, like, this chaos, right? Just like Iraq before that. And Afghanistan. You take out them dictators and the people who come in ain't got no clue what to do. Makes things worse in a way, you know?"

Marcus nodded slowly. He knew exactly what the man meant. The dissolution of the Cartel, however nasty and oppressive they were, had led to a power vacuum.

"So who's in control?" Marcus asked.

The man chuckled. "Man, you been under a rock or something? Really, you got no clue?"

Marcus looked at the man without blinking, purposely expressionless.

"Ain't nobody in *control*," said the man, shaking his head for effect. "You got a bunch of gangs that rule territories, manage black markets and such. It's like a real Wild West out here. Ain't no rules, nobody to keep nobody safe. Every man for himself. It's a dog eat—"

"I get it," Marcus cut in.

"So who's your somebody, then?"

Marcus surveyed the room. Nobody was paying attention to them. Each table was preoccupied with their own conversations and drinks. Marcus sighed and looked at the backs of the man's hands on the bar. No tattoos.

"You know anything about a gang that has dollar signs on their hands?" he asked.

The man's eyes twitched and he scratched his face along either side of his crooked nose. He looked over his shoulder and inched closed to Marcus. "Everybody knows about the LRC," he said, his voice barely above a whisper. "The Llano River Clan."

"That's my somebody," said Marcus.

The man scratched his face again. He swallowed hard, his Adam's apple sliding up and down. He gripped his fingers on the edge of the bar.

"You know where they are," said Marcus. "You can help."

The man swallowed again and nodded without looking at Marcus. "I can help," he said softly. "But I ain't cheap for something like that. You sure you ain't got a different somebody?"

Marcus picked up his glass and took another sip. He licked his lips, transferring the burn to his tongue. The mash was less bitter the more he drank. It was sweeter now, with a hint of corn. He offered what was left of the drink to the crooked-nosed man. The man took it and drained the cup into his mouth, gulping it down.

"It's gonna cost you more than leftover 'shine," he said. "The LRC is a nasty bunch. They ain't from here, but they make their way through every couple of months. They're pillagers. And they run women."

"Run women?"

"They're traveling pimps," he said. "They take the weak young ones with them and drop them off in different places. The older ones or the particularly feisty ones get dead pretty quick."

Heat welled in Marcus's gut and spread through his body. His cheeks warmed; his muscles tensed.

The man's eyes softened with recognition and he frowned. "Oh, I get it."

Marcus took a slow, deep breath through his nostrils and exhaled. The surge of adrenaline slowed. "What will it cost?"

"The Springfield."

Marcus turned around to face the bar and the pair of rifles he'd set on it. He ran his hands along the Springfield's walnut stock. He'd already given up the Glock. Now the Springfield?

"How about the Remington?"

"I like the Springfield better," said the man.

"So do I," said Marcus. "I've got plenty of ammo for both. I'll give you more of it if you take the Remington."

The man reached for the rifle and Marcus grabbed his arm, glowering at him. "*After* you show me where to find them."

The man pulled back his hand, motioning almost imperceptibly over his shoulder. His eyes moved in the same direction.

Marcus followed the hint. At the far end of the room, a grungy man in a sweat-stained Stetson was at a table with four other men, playing poker. Empty glasses littered the table. Marcus couldn't see the others, but the man with the Stetson had the dollar sign on the back of his right hand. The five appeared oblivious to anything happening in the bar beyond their table.

Marcus swung back to the barkeep. "I'd like to buy that table a shot each. That's five shots. Let's say ten rounds."

"Let's say fifteen," gargled the keep.

"Deal," said Marcus. "Let them know it's from me."

"Sure thing. Just leave the ammo on the bar."

Marcus reached into his bag and fished out the fifteen rounds. He also took an extra five and, while the barkeep made his way to the table, quickly loaded them into the Springfield. He eyed the crooked-nosed man with a look that warned he should remain silent and slid the safety and the magazine cutoff into the right positions with his thumb.

He turned back in time to see the bartender pouring a shot of moonshine into each of the five glasses on the table. The old man looked over his shoulder and hooked a thumb at Marcus, drawing ten eyes toward the bar. Marcus offered a weak salute to the table. The man with the Stetson tipped his hat and swigged the shot.

"C'mon," Marcus told the crooked-nosed man. "Let's go."

"What?"

Marcus picked up both rifles and started his move toward the open door. "Follow me."

The man followed and Marcus made a point to avoid eye contact on his way to the exit. They were a few steps from it when the

Stetson-wearing gang member called out, "Hey, stranger. Stop right there."

Marcus had his back to the man. He worked to suppress a smile before he turned.

The man stood from his chair and picked up his handgun from the table. He started toward Marcus and his accomplice, his eyes narrow and focused.

"Thanks for the drink," he said. "What's your game?"

Marcus's eyebrows arched with faux innocence. "Game?"

Stetson sauntered across the room and stood a few feet from Marcus. The other men stood from their seats and joined him in the middle of the room. All of them were armed. None of them appeared thankful for the free drinks.

Those sitting at the tables between the gang members and Marcus slid from their seats and either moved toward the bar or scurried out the door. Although Marcus had a rifle in each hand, he wasn't in a position to fire either of them. For a moment he wondered if he'd overplayed his hand.

"A man who buys a stranger a drink is playing a game," said Stetson. "I don't like games. Do you like games, fellas?"

The men behind Stetson all shook their heads, snarling their agreement with Stetson. Marcus almost laughed at the absurdity of it all. It was straight out of a bad spaghetti western. All that was missing was the town clock striking twelve and Allessandroni strumming his guitar.

"I'm not interested in games either," said Marcus. "I noticed the tattoo on your hand. Figured I'd pay tribute."

The man glanced at the black dollar sign on the back of his right hand, aiming his handgun at Marcus. "What about my ink interests you?"

"You're part of LRC, right?"

Stetson's eyes narrowed and he tilted his head to one side. "Who's asking? I don't think I got your name."

"Marcus Battle."

"Battle?" Stetson laughed. "That's a stupid name."

The men behind him laughed and smirked in agreement.

"So is Barbas."

Stetson leveled his handgun at Marcus. The other men drew their weapons. The crooked-nosed man raised his hands above his head. He tried to back out of the room, but Marcus grabbed his arm.

"What did you say?" asked Stetson. "I know I didn't hear you right."

Marcus spoke slowly and clearly. "So. Is. Barbas."

A grin snaked its way across Stetson's face. "You a dissatisfied customer, Marcus *Battle*? Or did you find out your woman is more satisfied with what Barbas has to offer?"

Marcus bit down on the inside of his cheek. He studied the sneering grins of the other four men backing up Stetson and the weapons they had trained on him.

"I've got no horse in this race," said the crooked-nosed man. "I don't know this fella. Marcus Battle. I don't—"

Marcus spoke from the corner of his mouth. "You might want to keep quiet."

"I'm not keeping quiet while they kill us. I'm serious. I don't know you. I just met you. I—"

A single shot silenced the crooked-nosed man and dropped him to the floor. He was dead before his head slapped against the concrete and bounced.

Stetson shrugged and slid his weapon back to Marcus. "Nobody's loyal these days," he said. "And he was giving me a headache."

Marcus stood still, blood pooling around his boots. His expression was unchanged. "Where is Barbas?"

Stetson looked over one shoulder and then the other. "Not here. I think you have some—"

"Get down!" came a high-pitched voice from behind Marcus. Marcus ducked, set the Remington on the floor in the pool of blood, and flipped the loaded Springfield to his shoulder. He leveled the rifle at the crowd of gang members.

Stetson's eyes widened and his mouth dropped open, the last word trailing into a gurgle as he grasped at his neck with both hands. His gun fell from his hand and rattled onto the floor. The hilt of a throwing knife protruded from his throat. Marcus sighted on the man next to Stetson and pulled the trigger.

Another knife whizzed over Marcus's head and found the center mass of the man to the left of the dying Stetson, who dizzily staggered into the table in front of him.

The remaining two gang members returned fire unsuccessfully. Marcus worked the bolt and slapped a pair of shots into one of them, driving him back and dropping him.

The lone living LRC raised his hands above his head. "I'm empty!" he cried out, spittle flying. "I'm empty. Don't shoot! Don't shoot!"

"You gonna shoot him?" came a voice from behind Marcus. It was Lou. "Or you gonna let him go?"

Marcus, his weapon still trained on the man, didn't respond. His finger was on the trigger. The Springfield's butt was pressed tight against his shoulder.

Lou brushed past Marcus, sidestepping the blood, and walked over to Stetson's body. She pressed her hand against his face and used the leverage to pry the blade from his neck. She wiped the blade on his shirt as if she were frosting a cake before she tucked it away. She stepped closer to the man with the empty gun and crinkled her nose.

"I'm thinking you might want to tell him what he wants to know," she said to the man. "You already pissed your pants. No need to stay quiet on account of your dignity."

The man, whose hands trembled as he tried to keep them above his head, nodded. "What do you want?" he asked Marcus. "I'll tell you anything, including where you can find Barbas."

Marcus looked to his left. Nobody else in the bar was moving. He didn't figure any of them as threats. Still, he kept his rifle aimed at the man. Lou made her way to another dead man and used her boot for leverage to remove her knife.

"So where is he?"

"Oh," said the man. "He's not here. He's not in Abilene. He was, but he's not. He left a couple of days ago. Had a couple of women with him."

"Where did he go?"

"San Angelo, I think," said the man. "We got a place down there where we…"

"Where you what?"

The man looked at the floor and swallowed hard. "It's just business," he mumbled.

Marcus lowered his weapon and took two confident steps toward the cowering gang member. He stabbed his finger in the man's face and spoke through his gritted teeth.

"I'm gonna let you live," said Marcus. "That way you can go tell people who I am and what I want."

The man blinked, his body trembling. "You're Marcus Battle."

"I'm Marcus Battle," he said. "I'm looking for Barbas, a man named Cego, and another with a scar on his face. He's called Rasgado. You tell anyone you see I'm coming for them. I'm going to find them all. And when I do, they're going to wish they'd killed me east of Rising Star. You got that?"

The man nodded.

Marcus turned to the rest of the bar. "Everybody hear that?"

The room rumbled with the tacit understanding of those hiding under tables and pressed against the walls. None of them reached for their weapons or said anything untoward.

Marcus picked up the Remington and led Lou from the carnage. He crossed the asphalt. The two bouncers were dead on the dirt, on their backs, with gaping wounds at their necks. He rubbed his chin and turned to Lou.

"How'd you manage that?"

"A girl's got her ways," she said, "and you gave them my knives. I couldn't believe it. I rode up here on the horse and see those two buffoons fumbling around with my knives. I was sure you were dead."

"Why is that?"

"Because I figured there was no way you'd give up my knives without dying."

Marcus found his Glock on the ground, checked the magazine, and holstered it, changing his weight onto his good leg.

"I think Highway 277 is that way," he said, pointing ahead. "That'll lead us to San Angelo. Let's get the horse and head out."

"I think we have our pick of them," said Lou. She motioned past the bar to where she'd tied up their Appaloosa. There were four other horses nearby. Two of them looked healthy; the others were bony and looked diseased. Marcus limped toward one of the two healthier ones. It was a tobiano paint and nickered as Marcus approached.

"You take this one," he said to Lou. "He's a calm one. I'll take the Appaloosa."

"Why'd you tell all those people who you were and where you were going?" she asked. "You're giving the bad guys a chance to get ready."

Marcus nodded. "Maybe they'll be ready. But now I know they'll be scared. They'll be looking over their shoulders. They'll be wondering every second of every day when I'm coming. That trumps them being ready."

He helped Lou into the saddle. He untied the horse and she took the reins, guiding the horse back to the road. Marcus slid the Remington into the scabbard and mounted the Appaloosa. He took the reins and met Lou where she circled her horse in the street.

He'd eased to her side when a pair of men exited the bar. They waved their hands over their heads and called out to them, asking them to stop. Marcus kept his horse walking.

"Hey," said one of them, a middle-aged man with a thick beard that ran up his cheeks like a vine. "I heard you talk about Rasgado. Emilio Rasgado."

Marcus pulled on the reins and eased the horse to a stop. "Yeah?"

"He's not Llano River."

"Neither is Cego," said the other, a skeleton of a man with rosy cheeks and buck teeth. His mouth didn't quite close all the way.

"They got their own gangs," he said. "They only run with Llano River sometimes."

"Rasgado deals dope," said the first man. "He'll kill a man who shorts him without blinking. He's the meanest son of a—"

"Where is he?" asked Marcus.

"I think he's still in town," said the man, his mouth barely visible behind his beard. "He's got a place he keeps near the old country club on the south side of town. Go a block and take 83 Business south. There's still a couple of signs that'll point you in the right direction."

"And Cego?"

"I don't know," said the bucktoothed man. "I just know he's not from here. We hear he's a coyote."

"A coyote?" asked Lou. "What's that?"

"A smuggler. He moves people back and forth across the wall."

Marcus huffed. "The wall, huh?"

"That's what I heard."

"Thanks," said Marcus. "We'll find him."

He loosened his grip on the Appaloosa's reins and clicked his teeth, kicking his heels into the horse's sides. The animal responded and resumed its walk.

"Hey," said the man with the beard. "If you don't die, come back and help us."

"We need somebody like you around here," echoed the

bucktoothed man. "There's good people in this world who need help."

Marcus nodded. "We'll see how it goes," he said and urged the horse forward. Lou followed and they took the road to the intersection with 83 Business. There was a sign pointing south.

"So we're going to a drug dealer's compound?" asked Lou, pulling the paint even with the Appaloosa. "That the plan now?"

"That's where it starts for us," said Marcus, "and ends for Emilio Rasgado."

Chapter 7

OCTOBER 22, 2042, 6:06 PM
SCOURGE +10 YEARS
SOUTH ABILENE, TEXAS

The sun hung low, threatening to drop beneath the uneven horizon. Marcus felt its warmth on his face as he and Lou led their horses past the building for the Knights of Columbus Council 2163. It was a single-story ranch with drooping power lines overhead and a railroad track beside it. The gravel parking lot appeared as though somebody had carpet-bombed it. Marcus weaved around the gaping holes, careful not to catch his horse's hooves.

Once they passed the building, he took them off-road and through the high grass of what was once the golf course on the north side of the Abilene Country Club. The horses seemed to appreciate the softer ground, nickering and sighing as they walked south toward the cluster of buildings ahead.

"Did you ever play golf?" asked Lou.

"Every once in a while," Marcus said, his eyes straight ahead. "I was just good enough to enjoy it and just bad enough not to care how I played."

Lou narrowed her eyes. "You don't look like a golfer."

Marcus chuckled. "What do I look like?"

Lou shrugged. "I don't know. You just look…sad."

The smile disappeared from Marcus's face. He tightened his grip on the reins, rubbing his thumbs against the leather straps. They clopped silently for twenty yards before Lou inched her paint closer to the Appaloosa.

"What do I look like?" she asked.

"That's a loaded question," Marcus said. "Let me think about it."

Lou rolled her eyes. "Cop-out."

Marcus smirked. "Maybe."

They moved farther south until they reached a steep upward slope to the left of a weed-ridden cart path. Marcus stopped his horse and signaled for Lou to do the same. The slope gave them enough cover to leave the horses and approach on foot. They were fewer than a hundred yards from a large parking lot framing the eastern edge of the compound.

Marcus tied both horses to a barren oak whose roots had worked their way through the cart path. He pulled the Remington from the scabbard and offered it to Lou.

She eyed him with apparent suspicion. "What about the empty one you gave me?"

Marcus jabbed it in her direction. "Take it. Your knives aren't going to be enough."

Lou took the Remington. "I told you I'm not good with these."

"You'll be good enough," Marcus said. "You have to be."

He took off his pack and laid it on the path next to the horses, walked back to the rise, and lowered himself onto his belly. He rested on his elbows and pulled his Springfield to his shoulder, looking through the scope and scanning the compound up ahead.

There was still enough daylight that he got a pretty good idea of the layout and where the trouble spots might be.

Directly ahead was a shell of an aluminum-framed building. The exterior walls were rusted and peeling away from the frame; the roof had large gaps in it, like a quilt missing patches in the middle.

Beyond the building was a wide parking lot. On its left edge was a cluster of smaller buildings and a pool area. To the right edge of the lot, set farther back, were a pair of twin single-story buildings and some tennis courts. Between the courts and the pool area, centered at the back of the lot, was what appeared to be the main building.

Although the compound wasn't as heavily guarded as Marcus had expected it to be, there were three men patrolling the parking lot. Marcus watched them repeat their pattern for close to thirty minutes before he pulled his eye from the scope. Lou was lying on her back next to him, her eyes closed. She was snoring.

It wasn't a loud snore, more like an aggressive purr. And it was spiced with an angry mumbling that Marcus couldn't understand. Then she cried out, screaming from the midst of whatever nightmare haunted her sleep. Marcus nudged her shoulder and shook her until she woke.

She snorted and her eyes popped open. Her hand instinctively slid to her waist and drew a knife. Before Marcus blinked, it was an inch from his right eye. Her eyes blinked into focus and she relaxed, lowering the blade. She didn't apologize. Marcus didn't ask her to.

He lowered his eye to the scope. The safety and magazine cutoff were in the correct positions. He drew the first of the three guards into his sight and waited for the man to stop near the twin buildings in front of the tennis courts. When he did, Marcus slid his finger from the guard to the trigger and squeezed.

The shot exploded from the weapon, slamming the butt into his shoulder and blasting through the quiet air. It echoed across the shallow valley of the golf course and hit the guard center mass. He crumpled into a heap.

Quickly, Marcus worked the bolt and found the second guard. He was in front of the main building and had his weapon drawn. He searched for the source of the shot. Marcus exhaled and pulled the trigger a second time. The shot was true, slamming into the guard's chest beneath the weapon and between his arms. He stumbled back and fell to the ground.

Marcus shifted to his left, looking for the third guard. That man was supposed to be near the entrance to the pool. He wasn't there. Marcus picked his head up, looking for the man with his naked eye. It was too far. He lowered his head and looked again through the scope, scanning the length of the compound from right to left and back until a strobing flash and the accompanying rifle cracks of semiautomatic gunfire caught his attention.

He tightened the Springfield's butt against his shoulder and exhaled, slid his finger to the trigger, and pulled. The first shot hit the man in his shoulder, jerking him to one side. Marcus cranked the bolt, ejecting the spent cartridge, and then reversed the action to load the next round. As the target struggled with his wound, Marcus put another bullet in him. And then a third.

"That wasn't subtle," said Lou. "It's like you kicked the anthill."

She was right. The brief exchange was loud. Marcus had emptied his rifle and one of the men had unleashed an AR-15. More men would be coming.

"Over there." He pointed to the dilapidated metal building ahead of them. "Let's go."

Marcus pushed himself to his feet, grabbed his pack, and led Lou toward the building. By the time they'd reached an opening and had slid into the dank space, Marcus heard angry shouts echoing from the compound.

Marcus navigated his way through the empty building, hurrying to the exterior wall closest to the parking lot. Once he reached the wall, he dropped to a knee and fished a handful of cartridges from his pack. He opened the Springfield's bolt and loaded five rounds into the chamber.

"You want this one?" Lou asked, offering him the Remington.

"No. It's got a four-round capacity. This is five. And if I need it, I've got the Glock."

Lou inched closer to the wall and leaned into a gap between sheets of metal to peek through the thin opening. Still on one knee, Marcus made an adjustment to his scope and carefully slipped the barrel of his Springfield through an adjacent wall gap. Again he drew the weapon to his shoulder.

"I see four," said Lou. "They're looking for us."

Marcus nodded. "I see them."

"As soon as you fire, they'll know where we are."

"You've said that before."

"Yeah," said Lou, "and there were only two guys then. Now there are twice that many. You can't take out all of them before they unload on us."

Marcus looked over at Lou. "Then you need to help. Drop to a knee and mimic what I'm doing."

Lou swallowed hard and nodded. "Fine." She pulled the weapon tight to her shoulder and adjusted her grip, then slid the barrel through the wall gap in front of her.

The voices were getting louder. The men were in the parking lot, moving toward them.

"Don't put your finger on the trigger until you're ready to fire," Marcus instructed. "Then pull. Crank the bolt and then repeat."

"Just tell me when you're ready," she said. "I've got the two on the right. They're closer."

Marcus took aim. "Okay," he said softly, "I'll count from three. When I get to one, pull the trigger."

Lou grunted her understanding and pressed the rifle against her shoulder.

Marcus found the first of his two targets. He was a big man with a wide frame, an easy hit at less than a hundred yards. "Three. Two. One."

He pulled the trigger and a shot blasted toward the man, striking him in the gut. No sooner had Marcus fired that shot when the world around him exploded in flashes of light and deafening cracks of gunfire. Ignoring the cacophony as best he could, he fired another shot at the big man, striking him in the jaw and dropping him.

Marcus found his second target as a burning sensation radiated in his side. He ignored it and took out the approaching threat. He aimed to the right. There was a man within thirty yards of their position. He was squatted low as he moved, spraying everything in front of him with a swath of rapid gunfire. As Marcus took aim, the man spun awkwardly and dropped to the ground. His body convulsed a couple of times before falling still. The world was silent again except for the ringing in Marcus's ears.

He looked over at Lou. "I thought you said you weren't good with guns."

"I'm not," she said. "It took me four bullets. It would have only taken two knives."

"So you're a hustler."

"What's that mean?" asked Lou. She reached into Marcus's pack and reloaded the Remington without help.

"It means you make someone believe you're not good at something when you're really good."

She stood and slung the rifle over her shoulder. "So *that's* what I'm like," she said. "*Hustler.* Interesting."

Marcus smirked. He looked back through the wall gap. Nobody else was coming for them yet. He pulled the rifle back and tried to stand, but a pain in his side kept him on his knee.

He reached down and touched his damp shirt. A sharp bolt of pain exploded beneath his rib cage. He grunted and exhaled loudly.

Lou stepped toward him. "You okay?"

Cold sweat beaded on his forehead and his stomach lurched. "I think I got hit."

Lou's eyes blinked with worry. She grabbed Marcus's shoulder. "Lie down. Put your feet on your pack. I think you're going into shock."

Marcus leaned back on his elbows and then flat on his back. Lou slid the pack under his feet and pulled his shirt up above the wound.

"Ooh," she said. "That's gross."

"What?" asked Marcus, squeezing tears from his eyes as he pressed them closed. "What?"

"It's not a bullet," she said. "You've got a piece of the metal wall sticking out of your side. It's jagged and bleeding pretty bad."

"That's good," Marcus said. "Can you pull it out?"

"Can I?" Lou asked. "Yes. Should I? I don't know, I'm not a doctor."

"Open my pack," Marcus said through a clenched jaw. "Get the first aid kit. You're gonna need to do a little surgery. And you're going to have to be fast. I'm sure more men are coming."

He laid his head back against the concrete floor. Clamping his jaw tightly, he puffed his cheeks while breathing slowly in and out through his nose in expectation of the greater pain to come. As the rush of the gunfight dissipated, the fire at the wound intensified.

"Okay," Lou said. "Here goes."

Marcus held his breath and felt his flesh tear; a searing rush of punishment exploded and then subsided. There was pressure at the wound, the sound of plastic tearing, and then Lou's mumble as she affixed a bandage to his side. Sweat dripped into his eyes and he licked beads of it from the scruff above his upper lip.

"That's all I can do for now," said Lou. "I don't have time for stitches."

Marcus slid onto his elbows. There was a wide flesh-colored patch beneath his ribs and to the left of his navel. Lou was stuffing the first aid kit back into the pack at his feet. She plucked the canteen from its side, uncapped it, and handed it to Marcus, along with two packages of ibuprofen.

"Drink up," she said. "I think there's a couple more headed this way. You've got to get up and act like a man."

Marcus gulped a swallow of the warm water. "How wide is it?" he asked and took another healthy swig, tasting the sweetness of the minerals.

Lou held up her fingers, indicating the size of the wound. "It's not wide, but it's two inches long. You're gonna need to stitch it later. You know, once we kill Rasgado."

Lou adjusted the Astros ball cap on her head, swinging the brim around to the back. She wiped her hair from her face with both hands, tucking the long strands behind her ears. Her dark eyes almost glowed against the dark color of her skin.

Marcus took another drink and recapped the canteen. Lou grabbed the Remington, stood, and slipped the barrel through the wall between two jagged edges of a ripped joint.

She leaned forward at her waist, her shoulders out in front of her feet, and looked into the scope. She moved her shoulders as if tracking her target, and then the weapon kicked with a bang into her shoulder. Although it knocked her back an inch, she held the weapon level. She hurriedly worked the bolt and leaned in again. Another shot blasted. Then another.

Lou stepped back, pulling the barrel back through the opening. "Three bullets that time. Two men down. I think we need to get to that main house pretty quick though. Rasgado's not coming out, I wouldn't think. From my experience, the bad men always hide. They let the grunts do their dirty work."

Marcus was on his feet. He was light-headed, but the sweat was drying on his neck and back. "Seventeen?" he asked. He pulled on his pack and leaned on the Springfield.

Lou was reloading the Remington. "Seventeen what?"

"Years old," said Marcus. "You're only seventeen. You don't act that young."

"My dad used to say everybody ages in dog years nowadays," she said. "By that count I'd be one hundred and nineteen years old. You'd be...Methuselah."

Marcus chuckled and moved slowly toward an opening in the side of the building. He was building up his momentum, each step a little easier than the one before it.

"You know about Methuselah?" he asked.

"My dad used to tell me stories at night."

Lou beat him to the opening and stepped out into the grass. She slung the Remington across her back, its strap running diagonally from one shoulder to the opposite hip, and withdrew her knives, holding both of them in her left hand.

It was virtually dark now. Only a purple and orange halo glowed against the horizon to their right.

Crouched low, the two of them crossed the parking lot, hugging its edges. There were bloodied bodies and weapons scattered on the asphalt. The wide lot narrowed to a driveway that squeezed between a building to their right and a pair of swimming pools to their left. One was circular, the other was rectangular, and both were empty.

The building on the right looked like it had once been the clubhouse and was now maybe a guardhouse or storage room. Three of the guards were dead on the ground in front of it.

Marcus and Lou worked their way past the driveway to a second wider parking lot. At the back of that lot was the compound where Marcus believed they'd find Emilio Rasgado.

As they drew closer, what they'd thought was a complex of buildings appeared to be one large structure. It was mostly clay red brick with a healthy band of Texas limestone wrapping its base from one end to the other. At the center of the large building were two rows of rectangular brick columns that led to the main entrance.

To its left was a curved wall with three large six-panel glass windows. Unlike most of the buildings Marcus had seen over the past decade, all of the windows were intact. Dim light flickered from the inside. There was movement that intermittently obscured the glow.

Marcus and Lou stayed low, hiding themselves behind the thick trunk of a dead ornamental tree on an island in the center of the parking lot. Marcus drew the Glock from its holster and checked the magazine before palming it back into the grip.

Lou pointed at the building with her knives. "You know this is stupid, right?" she said. "Busting in there without knowing what we'll find."

Marcus pulled back the Glock's slide to confirm there was a round in the chamber. "You don't have to go."

Lou sighed. "That's not what I'm saying."

"What *are* you saying?"

"You have a death wish."

Marcus tightened his grip on the Glock and adjusted the Springfield's strap across his chest. Sweat bloomed on his brow and he clenched his jaw. He glanced at the bay window and back at Lou. She was probably right. He didn't have much of a plan other than employing violent abandon. He wasn't being tactical or using what he'd learned in the military.

He wasn't being stupid though. He wasn't even being careless. Marcus knew, as he hid with a teenaged smart-ass behind a decaying tree in the parking lot of a defunct, overgrown golf course, his sole purpose was to exact revenge on those who'd wronged him. If it meant he died in trying to dole out his punishment, so be it.

It was skewed logic, but Marcus was skewed. His warped sense of reality had long strayed from anything the pre-Scourge Marcus recognized, let alone justified.

He was a shell of his former self. He'd twice lost his family. He'd helped kill Rufus Buck, the man whose life he'd risked his own to save so many years before. He'd spent half of the last decade alone and wandering the dark corners of his own mind. He'd named his weapons and had talked to ghosts. He was borderline psychotic and a young girl was calling him out.

Marcus stood and leaned against the tree, hitching from the instant throb that webbed from his newest injury. He blew out a heavy breath that carried with it the stress of the moment and he smiled at Lou.

"What would your dad say about me having nothing to lose, running in there with my guns blazing? What would he say about me killing a man who took my wife and children?"

Lou crept around the side of the tree, using the trunk to stand up. She nodded. "He'd say, 'What are you waiting for?'"

Marcus winked at Lou and marched with purpose toward the bay window to the right of the main entrance. Lou was a step behind and to his right.

"Your left!" Lou shouted.

Marcus whipped around in time to see two men emerging from between the columns. They were no more than twenty feet from him, but before they could take aim with their cumbersome rifles, Marcus had powered multiple shots into both of them. He stopped in front of the bay windows and looked to his right.

"Watch it," he said to Lou and leveled the Glock at the glass. Two more shots and the window exploded.

Marcus put his hand on Lou's back and urged her ahead of him at the open windows, keeping his eyes on the interior, searching for threats. Together they avoided the remnant shards of glass and climbed into the building. The odor hit them immediately.

Lou wrinkled her nose. "What is that?" she whispered.

"Weed."

"Weeds?"

"No," said Marcus. "Pot. Marijuana."

The flickering candlelight wasn't coming from the large dining room they'd just entered. It was from a hallway to their left and reflected in a large mirror behind a bar. The shelves on either side of the mirror were empty. The few tables left in the room were working stations for a drug operation.

Despite the drought and apparent lack of widespread power, Rasgado appeared to be managing a healthy marijuana business. There were scales on one table, mounds of dried cannabis leaves on another, and mortars and pestles on a third. The work was clearly unfinished. He and Lou must have interrupted the men.

Marcus passed the tables and spun left, both of his hands on the

Glock's grip as he turned toward the wide hallway that led from the dining room/drug den to the main lobby. Facing the entrance and against the wall was a long, narrow table that held a collection of candles.

"Which way are we going?" asked Lou, carrying one knife in each hand.

Marcus motioned toward the candlelight and moved cautiously toward the lobby. Once there, he could see the main entry doors were open. A body lay on the ground not far from the building. Moving through the lobby, he felt the warmth of the candles on his right side. Past the flickering light, there was another large room and a hallway leading to the right. The room appeared empty.

Marcus turned into the hallway, leaving the flickering light behind him and moving deeper into the darkness. He slowed his pace, inching forward while his eyes adjusted to the dimness of the room.

Lou was behind him and to his right. She was breathing heavily through her mouth and kept bumping into his pack. They were on carpet. Other than Lou's respiration, the pair moved in muted silence.

Once his eyes adapted to the lack of light, the gray outline of closed doors on either side of the hallway materialized. He kept his focus on the gap between the bottoms of the doors and the carpet. There was nothing of interest until they reached a T-intersection with a hallway that ran parallel to the front lobby, stretching from one end of the building to the other.

Marcus looked to his left. Darkness. He looked to the right and saw something. About twenty feet ahead, on the right side of the hallway, there was a dim yellow glow coming from beneath a closed door. He held a finger up to his lips then pointed at the light. Lou nodded. Ignoring the aching throb in his leg and the jabbing burn at his ribs, Marcus adjusted his grip on the Glock and slowly crept toward the narrow, horizontal beam of light.

He stepped past the door and pressed himself against the wall as much as he could with a pack and rifle on his back. He put the Glock in his left hand and extended his right toward the handle on the opposite side of the door. Lou stood directly in front of the door, knives at the ready.

When Marcus was about to turn the handle, the percussive crash of another door flying from its hinges came from behind Lou, throwing her body forward and slamming her awkwardly into Marcus's arm. Before he could process what had happened, a figure emerged from the opening across from him. In the dark, Marcus couldn't make out who the man was, but he was tall and he was armed.

Lou moaned softly on the ground. The man across the hall roared with anger and fired a shot point-blank at Marcus, trimming his ear and drilling a hole into the drywall next to his head. A second shot grazed his neck.

Marcus instinctively slid to one side, flinching from the shot, and returned fire with the Glock. The deafening blast of semiautomatic gunfire rang in his ears as he pulled the trigger again and again.

The dark figure jerked and convulsed against the repeated hits. He dropped his weapon and it rebounded at Marcus's feet. The combatant sank to his knees, sliding back against the open doorjamb. He was wheezing, his breaths shallow and full of blood. Marcus had heard the sound before. The man would be dead within a minute.

Ignoring the dying man, Marcus reached over for Lou. She shrugged him off, insisting she was fine. She picked up her knives and used the wall to balance herself as she stood. Marcus then opened the door next to him. Candlelight flooded the section of hallway where they stood.

The man across from them was already gray. Blood leaked from his mouth and ears. His torso was riddled and soaked. His gloved hands were limp at his sides, his long, angular face decorated with a long scar.

Marcus took a big step across the hall and squatted in front of

Emilio Rasgado so the man could see him. He grabbed Rasgado's jaw and pulled the dying man's eyes to his.

"I'm Marcus Battle," he said. "You killed my family east of Rising Star. You thought I was dying and you said I wouldn't even make it to lunch."

Rasgado's eyes fluttered and Marcus slapped him across the face. He reached around the man's neck and gripped it, pulling Rasgado's face closer to his, and hissed, "I made it."

Rasgado coughed, splattering blood across Battle's face. The dying man smiled. "Your woman," he gurgled. "I remember. She was…she was…" His muscles tensed; then his body went limp. His head fell to one side, resting on Marcus's forearm.

Marcus let go of Rasgado's neck and shoved the dead man to one side. He took a deep breath and stood, his injured leg screaming with pain.

"You're bleeding again," Lou said. She was standing against the wall.

Marcus reached for his ribs.

"Not there," she said. "Your neck and the side of your head."

Marcus touched his ear. His fingers came away bloodied. He wiped it on his shirt and touched the wound on his neck. It was superficial.

"I'm fine," he said. "Flesh wounds."

"You're not fine."

Marcus stuffed the Glock into his holster. "Let's go. We need to find a place to crash before we head south to San Angelo."

Chapter 8

OCTOBER 23, 2042, 7:31 AM
SCOURGE +10 YEARS
SOUTH ABILENE, TEXAS

A bird chirping woke Marcus from his restless night's sleep. He was flat on his back in a bunker at the southeastern edge of the Abilene Country Club, and when he tried to sit up, his inability to do it reminded him of the fresh sutures at his ribs.

He'd done them himself before passing out from exhaustion. Lou was still asleep, her jaw slack as she breathed in and out through her mouth, using the pack as a pillow.

The horses had been tied to a light pole at the tennis courts nearby the night before. Marcus rolled onto his side. They were still there, both grazing on the brittle grass and weeds that surrounded them.

Marcus slowly raised himself onto one knee and then to his feet. He puffed his chest to arch his back and work the stiffness from it. There wasn't a part of his body that didn't hurt. He rubbed his shoulders where the pack wore on them, touched his neck and the bandage he'd slapped on it.

He took a couple of steps up the slope of the bunker and onto the dewy grass that crept along the dirt in search of sunlight and water.

He found the water twenty yards south, a small pond that miraculously wasn't dry. Marcus fetched the filtering bottles and headed toward the pond's edge. His healing leg was disagreeable in the morning chill, but he forced it along to the water and back.

By the time he'd filtered a canteen full, Lou was awake. After adjusting her clothes and retying her shoes, she opened up the pack and pulled out a couple of bags of potato chips. She tossed one at Marcus and pulled open one for herself.

"Where'd you get these?" he asked.

"You're welcome."

"Thank you."

She popped a chip in her mouth and crunched on it. "I got a bunch of stuff," she said. "After you fell asleep, I snuck back into the building. They had boxes of old snack foods and cereals. I took some pot too. You never know when we could trade it."

Marcus ripped open the bag and sniffed the contents. It smelled like vinegar-flavored potato chips. He plucked one from the bag and placed it on his tongue, working it between his teeth and chewing it.

"Not the best," she said. "But potato chips don't go bad. Neither does dry cereal if it's sealed. It just gets really stale."

Marcus pulled a couple more salty chips from the bag. "I thought this stuff could only last a few months," he said. "Maybe the vinegar helped preserve them."

Lou shrugged. "Or all of the chemicals they put in them. Could be either. Or both."

Marcus looked at the bag. "The expiration date was January 2034. We're going to get sick."

"If we survived the Scourge, potato chips aren't going to kill us."

Marcus chuckled. "We need to hit the road."

The two of them finished the chips, packed up the horses, and headed south. Hanging from the side of the paint was a short rope looped through a pair of AR-15s. Marcus had added a half-dozen loaded magazines to his pack, which was now almost too heavy to carry. But leaving all of the weapons and extra ammunition would have been a fool's move.

The sunrise was partially obscured by a thin haze of clouds that tracked slowly across the sky. Lou kept her paint even with Marcus's Appaloosa. They rode south on 277 for nearly an hour and barely spoke. It was getting colder. Marcus pulled his denim collar up around his neck, being careful not to rub it against his newest wound. The clouds were thickening.

"So we were talking about the Scourge," said Lou.

Marcus unhooked the canteen and handed it over to her. "Were we?"

Lou rode easy in the saddle, her body loose and swaying with the movement of the animal. She looped the reins around the saddle horn while she uncapped the container and took a drink. She screwed it closed and handed it back to Marcus.

"What happened to you?" she asked.

"When?"

"After the Scourge. You're on this mission or whatever it is, like you lost your family yesterday. So I'm guessing everybody survived the pneumonia?"

Marcus ran his thumbs along the reins. He sucked in a deep breath to give him more time to think about how to answer her. There was no easy explanation, no one sentence that could ward off the barrage of questions that were sure to come. He held his breath for an extra beat and then let it out.

"I lost two families," he said.

"You a...what's it called?...a poolygamash?"

"Polygamist."

Lou snapped her fingers and pointed at Marcus. "Right. You one of them?"

"No."

"I don't get it, then."

"I was married before the Scourge," he explained. "We had a son.

He was a few years younger than you are now. He got sick, so did my wife. They didn't make it much past the first wave of infections in this part of the world."

Lou lowered her eyes. "Oh. I'm sorry."

"Thanks."

"What happened after they died?"

Marcus sighed. "Nothing. I kept to myself. I watched a lot of movies. I slept a lot. I killed just about anyone who wandered on to my land."

"Where was that?"

"East of Rising Star," he said. "I had a good piece of property. Power, water, fresh food, you name it."

"Power? How? My dad said almost nothing had power once the plants shut down."

"Natural gas generators," said Marcus. "They were hooked into a well on my land. I also had solar panels on the roof of the house."

"What happened?"

A stiff breeze blew across the road. Lou held onto her ball cap and lowered it on her head.

"About five years ago," Marcus said, "a woman was being chased onto my land. Normally I would have killed her and the men chasing her. For some reason, and to this day I don't know why, I helped her."

"Then you married her?"

"Not exactly. Her son was kidnapped. She asked for my help, and I agreed. Long story short, we ended up back at my place with her boy and another kid, a little girl."

"Who was the other kid?"

"You heard of the Dwellers?"

Lou shifted in her saddle away from Marcus, her jaw tightening. She nodded.

"Well," he said, "we had teamed up with them to stop the Cartel. Then the Dwellers backstabbed us. We were going to cross the wall and go north. Along the way, the kid's mom died. We decided to take care of her. We came back south and went back to my home."

"You fought against the Cartel?"

"Yeah."

"And the Dwellers?"

"Sort of. More like we ran from them."

Lou ran a hand along the brim of her cap and tilted it back on her forehead. "Then what?"

Marcus turned from Lou and looked south along the road ahead. It narrowed to infinity, as if the path ahead were endless. Or pointless. He rubbed his eye with his index finger knuckle.

"We were happy," he said wistfully. "It was like…like I had a second chance to make things right. It was me and Lola and Sawyer and Penny. We were a good little family, I think."

"Lola? Was she the woman you saved?"

"Yeah," Marcus replied, "but more it was her who saved me. I'd kinda gone off the deep end after my wife and son died. Being alone for so long, you lose yourself. Lola dragged me back from the abyss."

"And Sawyer?"

"Good kid. Smart. We'd go camping and hunting. He'd help me with maintenance around the property. There was always a lot to do."

"Penny was the kid you took in?"

"She was," said Marcus. "Sweet little girl. She was a baby. I don't know if she really remembered her real mother. We were the only family she knew."

"Sounds nice," said Lou.

"It was."

Lou lowered her voice and leaned back toward Marcus. "And then it wasn't?"

"And then it wasn't."

Marcus let his answer hang in the deepening chill of the air. He'd said enough. It was more than he'd given himself since the bandits raided his home and took everything from him.

His muscles tensed as he relived the attack in his mind. He remembered the changing sound of Lola's scream. It was defiant at first, laced with moxie and anger. Then it devolved, morphing into more of a cry for help and a simultaneous resignation that help wasn't coming fast enough. It was the kind of wail that made Marcus want to cover his ears and crawl into a hole.

He could still see Sawyer drop from the treehouse and feel the percussion of the sickening, muted thud his body made when it hit the ground. The boy's frightened, dead eyes stared back at him, asking Marcus why he hadn't been there to help him.

And Penny. He couldn't go there. Not Penny.

"Hey!" Lou snapped. "You there?"

Marcus blinked from his trance and stared at Lou, not focusing on her at first. He was still in Rising Star, reliving the nightmare.

Lou leaned over until her eyes met Marcus's. "I've been talking to you," she said. "You went somewhere else."

"Sorry," Marcus said. "Just thinking."

"I asked you if you have a plan for this next one. We're riding all the way to San Angelo. What's gonna happen when we get there?"

Marcus scratched his head and ran his hand across his forehead, squeezing his temples. "Other than killing?"

"Yeah."

"Nothing," said Marcus. "Why would there be anything other than that?"

Lou shrugged. "I guess there wouldn't be. You're a one-trick pony as far as that's concerned. All killing all of the time."

"I didn't kill you."

"You're my hero," said Lou.

He looked at Lou and noticed a three-inch scar across her neck he hadn't spotted before. It was faded but there. He stared at the raised, jagged mark and wondered how he hadn't seen it. It reminded him he didn't know the girl at all. His gut panged with regret for having opened up to her. She was a virtual stranger. The weight he'd removed by sharing his story with her sank back onto his shoulders.

"I'm nobody's hero," Marcus deadpanned.

Lou rolled her eyes. "I was being sarcastic."

"I wasn't."

"My dad used to say—"

Marcus held up a hand. "Look," he said. "I'm not interested in one of your dad's pearls of wisdom right now. I want to focus on getting to San Angelo. I want to get there and find Barbas, and I want to kill Barbas. That's what I want right now."

"I—"

"You *what?*" snapped Marcus. "You have something bitingly insightful to add? Grow up, Lou. This world is simple. It's black and white. If you're not the one doing the killing, somebody's killing you. If you don't like my take, if you'd rather cling to your father's treatise on life, be my guest. But don't slow me down, don't question me, and don't judge me."

Lou closed her slack jaw and sat up in her saddle. She pulled her shoulders back and looked straight ahead, pulling the horse to the left, moving the paint as far from the Appaloosa as she could while keeping her animal on the road.

For an instant, Marcus thought about apologizing for his outburst. She was only a kid, after all. But he didn't. She needed to understand who was in charge. She had to know that Marcus Battle wasn't a hero. He wasn't going to save her. She had to understand his purpose in life, as it were. There wasn't going to be a happy ending.

Chapter 9

OCTOBER 23, 2042, 5:31 PM
SCOURGE +10 YEARS
SOUTH BLACKWELL, TEXAS

To the right of Highway 277, north of where it merged with Highway 70, Marcus spotted a cloud of blackbirds circling at various elevations. He scanned the land between the cloud and the highway.

Close to him, lining the road, was a thin line of trees. Some of them were still green, though most were brown and dry. Through the thinning canopy, he could see a clearing, and beyond that the topography leveled out. He reached for his canteen and shook it.

"There could be some water over that way," he said.

Lou, who was still walking her horse a couple of lengths ahead of Marcus, didn't turn around. She tilted her head back and looked up at the birds, squinting.

"We should head over there," he said. "We're out of water again."

"Whatever," Lou said and guided the paint toward the tree line. "You're the boss."

Marcus eased the Appaloosa off the road, moving the horse parallel to Lou's. They wove their rides amongst the trees, the sound of pine needles and dead leaves crunching underneath the animals' hooves.

"I shouldn't have talked to you the way I did," Marcus said.

Lou ignored him.

"It's not an apology," Marcus clarified. "The intent was good; the delivery was bad."

Lou glared over her shoulder. "Apology accepted."

"I said—"

She pulled her cap from her head, mopped her brow with the back of her forearm, and slid the hat back on. "I know what you said, Marcus."

"I don't want you thinking I'm going to save you," he said. "I'm not some answer you've been seeking. I'm not a good man. Not really. I can't be your family."

Lou pulled sharply on the reins and stopped her horse between two spindly pines. She adjusted her weight in the saddle, her brow furrowed and her mouth curled downward into a frown. "What makes you think I want any of that from you?" she blasted. "You forced *me* to follow *you*, remember? You took my knives. I had no choice."

Marcus rubbed the back of his neck and looked at the ground. She was right.

"I don't need you to save me," she said, "and I don't need a family. My dad was my family."

"You're right," said Marcus. "I shouldn't have assumed anything."

"You're the one who's craving family, Marcus, whether you want to admit it or not."

Marcus flinched. "That's where you're wrong," he scoffed.

Lou clicked her teeth and kicked her heels into the horse's sides. "Keep telling yourself that," she said, and trotted the paint west toward the clearing beyond the trees.

Marcus took a deep breath, which he stored in his cheeks for a moment, then puffed out through his mouth. He directed his horse to follow Lou. There was no point in arguing with her. There'd be time for that later, he was sure.

He guided the horse through the woods, aiming for the clearing, when Lou stopped short ahead of him. He pulled on his reins. "Whoa," he said to the Appaloosa.

Lou looked over her shoulder and whispered, "I see the water."

"Then why did you stop?"

"There's somebody there," she said. "He's got a horse and a dog."

"Is he armed?"

"I can't tell," she said. "Isn't everybody?"

Marcus swung his good leg over the saddle and lowered himself to the ground. He walked his horse forward to Lou and handed her the reins.

"So I'm waiting here?" she asked.

"I'm not going anywhere."

Marcus slung the Springfield from his back and shrugged off the pack. He lowered the heavy bag to the ground and rolled his shoulders forward. He almost felt weightless without the pack.

He stepped to the edge of the tree line and dropped to a knee. He made sure the safety was flipped on and kept his finger outside the trigger guard. Marcus aimed the weapon's scope toward the water and found the man at its edge.

His back was to Marcus and he was bent over the water. To his left was a large horse, a thoroughbred, and to his right a mutt.

The dog wagged its tail as the man turned and offered it water from his cupped hands. The animal looked like a terrier mix. It had been a long time since Marcus had seen a dog. Aside from a few wild packs, he thought all of them had become last resort delicacies.

Marcus scanned the length of the lake's edge. The man was alone, aside from the grouping of birds pecking at something dead at the southern corner of the water. As Lou suggested he would be, the man was armed. There was a shotgun in a scabbard on the side of the horse. He also had a holster at his hip, a thick leather belt strapped across his back, and a shotgun shell belt draped across his torso like a sash.

The man rubbed the dog's head and behind its ear. The dog stretched its neck to lick the man's face.

Marcus walked back to Lou. "He can't be all bad," he said. "His dog likes him."

"So you're not going to kill him?"

"Not yet," said Marcus. "Let's measure him first."

"Can't we just avoid him and keep moving? We can find water somewhere else."

"Too risky," said Marcus. "We need water and so do the horses."

"What's your plan?"

Marcus held up a finger and then walked back to the edge of the tree line. He hid behind the thickest trunk he could find and pulled the rifle to his shoulder.

"Hey!" he called out, his voice echoing across the clearing. The man almost lost his footing, stumbled back, and immediately reached for his hip.

"Don't do it," Marcus said. "We've got you surrounded. Put your hands up."

The man hesitated but raised his hands. "I don't have anything but the horse," he said. "You can take the horse."

The man's eyes were wide with fear, darting along the tree line. The pearl-handled six-shooter in the man's pocket was strapped tight. He hadn't been fast enough to even unlatch the snaps. His chin trembled.

"Take a couple of steps forward!" yelled Marcus.

The man complied and stepped away from the horse. He kept his hands in the air above his head, his eyes sweeping the tree line. The dog moved even with the man, wagging its tail.

"A couple more steps," Marcus called. "Then slowly, and I mean *slowly* unsnap that pistol and toss it toward the horse. Any funny business and the dog gets it."

Lou snickered. "Funny business? Who talks like that?"

The man complied quickly. He tossed the gun to the horse. The thoroughbred, drinking from the pond, picked up its head at the noise and glanced toward the man, and dipped its muzzle back into the water.

"Don't shoot my dog," he said. "Please. Take the horse. Whatever you want."

"Lie down on the ground on your stomach," Marcus said, his voice echoing. "Hands on the back of your head."

The man did as Marcus told him. Again he pleaded, "Please don't hurt the dog."

Marcus backed away from the tree line and lowered his weapon. He took the reins from Lou and climbed back onto the Appaloosa. Lou frowned.

"You could share with me what we're doing," she said. "It would make everything a lot easier. We *are* in this together."

"Fine," Marcus said. "Get on your horse. We're going to get our water and find out more about this guy."

"I don't think he's a threat," said Lou.

"Everybody's a threat."

"Not necessarily. There's the bad people who need killing. Good people need to be left alone. There *are* good people who survived the Scourge. Only the bad ones are the threats."

"Two days ago you tried to kill me," said Marcus. "Was I a threat?"

Lou spun the Astros ball cap on her head, adjusting the brim so it was facing forward. "You yourself told me a few hours back you were not a good man. Remember?"

"I remember."

Lou spurred her paint forward and they walked their horses closer to the man. Marcus had his Springfield perpendicular to the saddle, holding it flat on his thighs and against the horn. The man didn't move as they got closer. The dog, however, stopped wagging its tail. Its shoulders squared and a patch of hair on its back stood up straight. The dog backed closer to the water's edge and then moved toward the man on the ground. Its teeth were bared and it snarled a warning for Marcus and Lou to keep their distance.

Marcus and Lou stopped their horses a few feet from the man and his four-legged posse. He scratched his itchy neck and sighed. "How's the water?" he asked.

The man's voice was muffled. His face was in the dirt. "What?"

"How's the water? We don't want trouble. We just want water."

The man picked up his head, arching his back. "Seriously?" he asked incredulously, the tremble gone from his voice. "Water?"

"We're thirsty," said Lou.

"You could've asked," said the man. "Sheesh."

"We don't know who you are," said Marcus.

"Rudy Gallardo. Can I sit up, please?"

Marcus glanced over at Lou and back at the man on the ground. "Sure. But no fast moves and don't sic that dog on my horse."

Rudy moved himself into a sitting position and crossed his legs. He held his hands up.

"You can put your hands down," said Marcus.

Rudy lowered his hands. "Fifty," he said to the dog. *"Siéntate!"*

The dog sat on its haunches, relaxed its muzzle, and wagged its tail. Its wary glare, however, remained fixed on Marcus.

"Fifty?" asked Lou. "That's your dog's name?"

Rudy palmed the sweat from his brow and from under his eyes. He nodded. "Yeah. He's fifty percent pit bull, fifty percent who knows what."

Lou smiled. "I like it."

Rudy didn't smile. His light brown skin was painted with the brushstrokes of too much sun. He had the marks of crow's feet at the corners of his eyes, but not from age. They were from squinting too much. He looked to be in his late forties but had a full head of jet-black hair. His face was speckled with salt-and-pepper stubble. His shirt was sweat stained at the collar and his blue jeans were worn beyond repair. He took another swipe at the sweat beading under his nose and shrugged.

The dog whimpered, licked its chops, and yawned.

"So what are we doing here?" Rudy asked. "You gonna hold me at gunpoint while you get water? I should be afraid of you more than you should be afraid of me."

Lou shot Marcus a smirk. "I told you," she said.

Marcus started to dismount the horse. He swung one leg over the saddle and the dog growled. Marcus stopped.

"*Silencio,*" said Rudy. The dog grumbled.

Marcus hopped from the horse. "I'm going to hold onto your weapons until we get to know each other a little better. But you're free to do whatever it was you were doing."

Rudy huffed. "Gee, thanks."

Marcus picked up the six-shooter and then took the shotgun from the scabbard at the side of the thoroughbred. He tucked the pistol into his waistband, slung the shotgun over his shoulder, and walked toward Rudy.

"I'm a lot less concerned about your feelings than I am about my survival," Marcus said.

Rudy squinted, his nose crinkled as if he'd smelled something sour. "Who are you?"

Marcus squatted, resting his butt on his heels. "Marcus. And this is Lou."

"Father and daughter?" Rudy asked.

"No!" Lou said emphatically. "I barely know him."

"Did you take her weapons when you met her?" Rudy asked.

Lou giggled. Marcus stood up, offered Rudy a hand, and pulled him to his feet. Rudy was average height and build with broad shoulders. His hands were calloused at the base of his fingers. He set his hands on his hips. There was a tattoo on his right forearm that read *Norma*. He eyed Marcus, then Lou.

"Are you okay?" he asked her, motioning toward Marcus with his head.

Lou furrowed her brow, seeming to consider the question before her eyes popped wide with understanding. She shook her head. "It's nothing like that," she said. "I'm fine."

Marcus stepped back from Rudy. "We're traveling partners, that's it. Not family, not…anything else."

Rudy scratched his chin. "Where are you going? Can I ask that?"

Marcus stepped backward toward his horse, keeping watch on Rudy. He shrugged off his pack one shoulder at a time and set it next to the Appaloosa, unzipped it, and withdrew the two filtering bottles.

"Where are you headed?" he asked, walking back to the water's edge. He took a wide berth around the dog and dipped a bottle in the water.

"San Angelo," Rudy replied.

"That's where we're headed," said Lou.

Marcus turned to glower at Lou. She winked at him.

Rudy's eyebrows arched with surprise. "Really? Why?"

"Marcus has some killing to do," Lou blurted.

Rudy's brow relaxed and he swallowed hard. "Oh."

Marcus pulled the bottle from the lake and stood. "It's not what you think."

Lou swung a leg over her saddle and dismounted, landing on the dirt with both feet, and ran her hand along the horse's mane.

"You don't know what he's thinking, Marcus," she said.

Rudy shook his head. "No, he probably does."

Marcus smirked. "You wanna get some sticks from over there?" he asked Lou. "We need to start a fire, get this water boiled."

Lou rolled her eyes and huffed but marched along the edge of the lake to gather kindling. Marcus set the shotgun on the ground next to his horse, grabbed the pot from his pack, and approached Rudy.

"Her dad died," he said. "We ran into each other. I took her knives but couldn't leave her defenseless, so she tagged along."

"Knives?"

"She likes knives."

"Sheesh," said Rudy. "You are a pair made in heaven."

Marcus shook the empty plastic bottle to loosen the activated carbon and started transferring the water into the folding camping pot. He processed Rudy's sentiment and smiled.

"Not sure about the heaven part," said Marcus. "You hungry?"

Rudy licked his lips. "Sure."

Marcus left the water bottles and walked back to his pack. He pulled out a trio of Twinkies and tossed one of them to Rudy. "These things last forever."

Rudy tore into the plastic and took a healthy bite. "Twinkies?" he asked while chewing. "I haven't seen one of these in years."

"Lou found them at our last stop," said Marcus. "We were in Abilene."

Rudy shoveled all but a small bite of the treat into his mouth. "Killing people there too, were you?"

"Yeah."

Rudy stared at Marcus.

Lou approached with an armful of sticks and dropped them at Marcus's feet. "Eating my snacks?"

Marcus handed her one. "Our treats."

Rudy made kissing noises at his dog and offered the last bite to the mutt, who gently tongued the morsel from Rudy's palm.

Marcus arranged the sticks and within a few minutes had a small fire blazing. He set the pot on top of the fire and started filling the empty bottle with more water.

Rudy confronted the elephant in the field. "Who is it you're killing?"

Marcus and Lou exchanged glances. "Bad people," said Lou. "He wants revenge."

"Revenge? For what?"

"Long story," said Marcus. "Suffice it to say, three men have it coming to them. One's already got it."

Rudy nodded. "In Abilene?"

"In Abilene," Marcus confirmed.

"I'm looking for revenge too," said Rudy. "Though I only have one name on my list."

Marcus's eyes widened with surprise. To this point, Rudy hadn't looked like the revenge type.

Lou was picking at her Twinkie, relishing every nibble. She licked some of the white cream from her thumb. "Who?"

Rudy stared into the growing flames, his gaze becoming distant. "I don't know his name. I know what he looks like and I know he's in San Angelo."

"What's he look like?" asked Lou.

"And how do you know he's in San Angelo?" asked Marcus.

Rudy spoke as if in a trance, as if some memory had control of him and the words were automated. "He has a fiery red beard and dollar tattoos on the backs of his hands. His voice sounds like a chainsaw."

A chill ran along Marcus's spine, the hairs on the back of his neck tingling. His pulse quickened. "Barbas."

Rudy tilted his head to one side. "What?"

"His name is Barbas," said Marcus. "We're looking for the same man."

Lou shoveled the remaining Twinkie into her mouth. "Well, isn't that a coincidence?"

"Wait, what?" asked Rudy. "Your guy has a red beard and tattoos and—"

"It's the same man," said Marcus. "Did he kill your woman?"

Rudy's eyes drifted to his feet. He rubbed his forehead with his hands. When he looked up again, his reddened eyes were glistening. His words weren't much more than squeaks. "No," he said. "He took her."

"Then how do you know it's him?" asked Marcus.

"What happened?" asked Lou.

Rudy swallowed hard and knuckled the tears from the corners of his eyes. He took a deep, ragged breath and exhaled. "I live in Baird. I mean, I did. I had a small place. Me, my wife, my two cousins Sal and Al, and Al's wife, Trina. There were five of us. Somehow we all survived the Scourge. We supplied hay to the Cartel, so they left us alone for the most part. Then the Dwellers let us be. In the last year or so we've been getting hassled on and off by whoever. I told everyone we should move, find somewhere farther off the highway. There are plenty of empty ranches everywhere. You can throw a rock and find one. They didn't listen. They were happy where we were. They thought we could hold our own."

Rudy's face was drawn with pain. As much as the sun had done to etch his face, sorrow had done more. Frown lines stretched from the corners of his mouth to the edges of his trembling chin.

"I wasn't there when it happened," Rudy said sadly. "I was fishing. Me and Fifty were maybe a half mile from our land. I'd stocked a pond with channel catfish a year before the Scourge. It's been feeding us pretty regular since then. Had some bass and some bluegill in there when I started it, but they pretty much went by the wayside. Only the cats kept propagating."

There was a twinkle of happiness in Rudy's eyes when he talked about the fish and the care he gave the pond. It was, if nothing else, a respite from the drudgery and relative misery of a post-Scourge existence. For Marcus, the garden had provided that momentary escape. He empathized with Rudy's need to tend the pond.

The twinkle disappeared as Rudy talked about returning to the ranch and sensing something was off. The dog had been whimpering, he said. The hair at the base of Fifty's neck was on end.

"I pulled my shotgun," he said, mimicking the act of holding the weapon waist high, "and I crept up slow to the house. The front door was off the hinges. One of the windows was broken. There was glass on the porch. So was one of my cousins. Sal was dead. There was blood pooled all around him."

Marcus pictured the unfolding horror in his mind. He put himself in Rudy's shoes, approaching the carnage with a mix of disbelief, angst, and bubbling rage. Lou was mesmerized, her large eyes fixed on Rudy as he told the story with his hands and facial expressions.

"I walked through the broken door into the house," Rudy said. "There's a long hallway there leading straight back to the kitchen. To the right there are stairs. I could see fresh dirty boot prints on the wood steps, and there were scratches in the wood and on the wall, like someone had dragged their fingernails. I started upstairs, but I heard moaning from the kitchen. It didn't sound human. Not really. But I knew it was. I knew it was my other cousin."

Rudy's hands were shaking, his eyes focused on some distant point. "He was still alive," he said. "Barely. He told me what happened."

Lou's hands were covering her mouth. "What happened?" she mumbled through them.

Rudy swallowed hard and absently ran his fingers along the sides of his face. "Al said a red-bearded man took our wives. He was with three or four other men. They had dollar-sign tattoos. He was shot in the stomach. It was bad. I tried to help him."

Rudy stared blankly into the distance. Lou and Marcus sat quietly. A breeze rippled across the lake and the nearby blackbirds squawked, flapping their wings.

Tears flooded Rudy's eyes and streaked down his face, running into the furrows along the sides of his mouth. "Al overheard them talking about San Angelo. There's a place there where they take the women. That's where I'm going. To get Norma and Trina."

"By yourself?" asked Marcus.

Rudy's eyes flashed with anger. "You're by yourself."

Lou cleared her throat.

"Sorry," Rudy apologized. "Still, it's just the two of you."

Marcus exchanged glances with Lou. He knew what she was thinking. As much as he didn't like the idea, it was a good one.

"You could join us," Marcus said. "We could get Barbas, and your wife and Trina. Together."

Rudy's eyes slid from Marcus to Lou and back to Marcus. He sniffed and wiped his nose with the back of his hand. "Do I get my guns back?"

"Once we're on the road," said Marcus.

Rudy grunted his agreement. "Fine."

Marcus took off his denim jacket, wrapped it around his hand, and pulled the boiling water from the fire. He drained the pot into the canteen, refilled it with a second bottle, and placed it back onto the fire. He looked at his two traveling companions and then the dog. Fifty was pushed against Rudy's body, wagging his tail.

"This is beginning to feel like *The Wizard of Oz*," said Marcus. "Before long we'll have flying monkeys chasing after us."

"I guess that makes you Dorothy?" Lou quipped.

Rudy eked a smile. "You're kinda young to know about that movie, aren't you?"

"I never saw the movie," said Lou. "My dad read me the book when we were holed up in a library. He read me a lot of things."

Marcus pulled an unburned stick from the edge of the fire. "Yeah? Like what?"

"Biographies," she said, "cookbooks, and some things he called classics."

Marcus took a roll of fishing line from his first aid kit and knotted a hook into the end. Then he tied it to the end of the stick and held it out to Rudy.

"Wanna fish?"

"We need to get going," said Rudy. "Every minute Norma and Trina are with that man is another minute they're in danger."

"It's already getting dark," said Marcus. "We're not going anywhere tonight. First thing in the morning we'll head out for San Angelo. We'll be there by nightfall tomorrow."

Rudy folded his arms across his chest. "I haven't fished since…"

Marcus jabbed the makeshift fishing pole in Rudy's direction.

"Now's as good a time as any."

Rudy took the pole. "I don't have any bait."

"Use a Twinkie," Lou suggested. "Maybe you draw a small fish you can cut up and use as bait for a bigger one."

"Read that in a book?" asked Marcus.

Lou grinned. "You'd be surprised by what I learned from books."

Marcus chuckled. "I'm sure I would."

Two hours later Lou was using one of her knives to fillet a trio of crappie. She told Marcus she didn't need any help.

"I can do it," she said, the first one in her bare hand, and split the fish from the top to behind its gills. She then took the knife and made a horizontal cut toward the back at the top and bottom of the fish, which helped her expose the fleshy meat of the fish. She peeled back the fillet and, starting at the tail, she slid the knife between the skin and meat to separate the two.

"You can leave the skin on mine," said Rudy. "It'll get crispy and make better eating. Plus, Fifty likes it that way."

"Ew," said Lou. "I don't like the skin. But fine, however you want it."

She used the knife's sharp front edge to trace around the rib cage and made the appropriate cut to remove the bones.

"I could split this into two," she suggested. "Or we could just make them thick."

"Cut them into two," said Rudy. "It'll be easier to cook, and we get two pieces each."

The three of them and Fifty soon ate their pieces of fish as if the meal were their last on Earth. Lou ate her pieces faster than the dog. Marcus praised her for her work and Rudy for his before he put out the fire for the night.

Without the ambient heat of the flames, it was markedly colder. Even as they moved the horses to the cover of the trees, the chill stayed with them. Marcus drew his collar up around his neck and buttoned up his jacket.

"Remind me why we didn't sleep inside last night when we had the chance?" asked Lou.

"Escapability," he said. "Didn't want to get stuck inside a closed space if things went sideways while we slept. Better to have three hundred and sixty degrees of movement available."

"I wish it were three hundred and sixty degrees," she said. "Then I might be able to sleep."

"Use leaves," said Marcus, lying on his back with one leg crossed over the other and his hands tucked under his pits. "Pile them up like a blanket. They'll insulate you."

"Don't do that," said Rudy. "It'll make a mess. Just use Fifty."

Rudy whistled at the dog and then snapped his fingers toward Lou. "*Acotarse*," he said. "Lie down."

The dog lapped at Rudy's face before padding the short distance to Lou. He sat next to her and sniffed her head. He licked the sweaty brim of the Astros cap and then lay down next to her, his body against hers.

"You can put your arm around him," said Rudy. "He won't bite. He's only mean when I want him to be."

Lou draped her arm over the dog and rubbed the soft fur at his chest. "Thanks," she said. "You're a nice man, Rudy. Good night."

"Good night, Lou," said Rudy. "Marcus, I want to be on the road before sunup."

"No problem, Rudy. Goodnight, Lou," said Marcus.

Lou rolled onto her back. "Goodnight, Dorothy."

Chapter 10

OCTOBER 24, 2042, NOON
SCOURGE +10 YEARS
BRONTE, TEXAS

Marcus wiped the sweat from the back of his neck and took another swig of water from the canteen. A green mileage marker on the side of the highway announced they were twenty-five miles from San Angelo.

"Is it me," asked Rudy, "or is it a lot warmer today?"

"It's definitely warmer," Lou replied. Fifty was riding in front of her on the large saddle. The paint had been wary at first, but acquiesced. "I guess you gotta be careful what you wish for."

They were in Bronte, Texas, a town somewhere between nowhere and nothing. Before the Scourge, the town had a population of nine hundred and seventy-four people. If there were nine hundred and seventy-four mosquitoes in the place now, Marcus would have been surprised.

A thick layer of grayish-yellow dust covered the road and most of the buildings that still stood. Most of them glass and brick, with hints of stucco here and there. A broken plastic sign swung from its perch in front of Long Branch BBQ. It was a ghost town. The trio worked their way south on Highway 277, which ran north and south straight through the center of Bronte. They were smack-dab in the middle of the town at State and Main, Bronte Hometown Hardware to their right, when Fifty's ears perked. The dog lifted its head and barked.

"What's wrong?" Lou asked.

"He's sees something," said Rudy. "Stop your horse so he can hop down."

Lou pulled on the reins, and the moment the paint stopped walking, the pit bull mix was on the cracked asphalt, the hair on his back sticking up.

Marcus tossed Rudy his shotgun. Rudy nodded his appreciation and quickly loaded the pump-action twelve gauge. Marcus pulled his Glock from his holster and held it in front of him in the saddle. Lou drew her knives.

The dog took a couple of steps forward. His ears pricked again and he growled. He was focused on a building ahead of them and to the right on the southwestern corner of the intersection, the first of a row of narrow buildings butted next to each other.

Rudy whispered something to his horse and hopped off. He walked over to Fifty. "What's going on, boy?" he asked, running one hand along the top of the animal's head. He held the shotgun in the other.

Fifty whimpered, his attention glued to the first building on the corner, his muscles tensed as if ready to pounce.

Lou balanced a knife in her right hand, her left gripping the reins.

Marcus let go of his reins and put both hands on the Glock's grip. He raised the weapon and leveled it at the building. The wind whistled through the streets, tumbling a large piece of crumpled cardboard from one side of Main to the other.

"Hey!" called a faint voice from inside the first building. "Don't shoot!"

"And don't sic that dog on us neither," said a stronger, deeper voice. "We ain't done nothin'. Ain't gonna do nothin'."

"The lady doth protest too much, methinks," Marcus said.

Bouncing the knife up and down in her hand, Lou said, "*Hamlet*, act 3, scene 2."

Marcus smiled.

A pair of hands appeared from an open wood casement window. They were thin with long fingers, waving wildly. "See?" said the deeper voice. "Nothin'."

"What do you think?" asked Lou. "Good people or bad people?"

"You know what I think," said Marcus. It was odd. This was an empty town, barely even a waypoint between Abilene and San Angelo. Most people would be on their toes and defensive. If threatened, they'd pull a gun first and not claim to be unarmed. Especially if they had no way of knowing someone already had the drop on them.

With his hand still on the mutt, Rudy motioned toward the building with his head. "I think they're okay. I don't see any weapons."

"I told ya," said the softer voice. "We're clean as a whistle."

"Let me see the backs of your hands!" Marcus called out. "Flip your hands around."

The hands disappeared into the building. "What?" called the deeper voice. "Why?"

"Let me see the backs of your hands," Marcus repeated.

Rudy pulled his hand from the dog and cupped it under the fore-end of his shotgun. He pulled the butt to his shoulder and thumbed off the safety behind the trigger. He was well within the fifty-yard range of his weapon.

Fifty edged forward on his haunches. His jaw squared and the hair on his back, which had relaxed, straightened again. The dog was alternately panting and offering a low growl.

"Okay then," said the deeper voice. The fingers of one hand appeared from the casement window, the dirt black fingernails, the rough knuckles, and then the dollar-sign tattoos. The man held them there for a moment, wiggling his fingers. "This good eno—"

The man disappeared from the window and wailed like a banshee. "My hand!"

Blood streamed from the center of the tattoo around the edges of a blade. His hand was stuck flat against the wooden casement, pinned there by Lou's knife. The man struggled vainly to withdraw the knife from his hand and the wood. He twisted his body awkwardly and a second man's torso emerged through the open window. He grabbed at the knife, trying to help his comrade, when a second blade silently spun through the air and speared the side of his neck. He convulsed and dropped over the window ledge, his body draped there while his nervous system twitched until he died.

Fifty sprang forward and raced to the wounded, crying man. He stopped at the window, bared his teeth, and snarled. The man raised his free hand above his head.

Marcus jumped from his horse and, with Lou and Rudy at his side, approached the wailing man. He looked young. His frightened eyes lacked the dull resignation of older, wiser men. His teeth were sparse, though, and drool leaked from his thin, cracked lips. He was pale and beads of sweat coated his bald head.

"Take it out!" he cried. "Take it out!"

Marcus shoved the dead man's body aside and climbed through the window. He slid his Glock into his holster, pulled a handgun from the man's waistband at the small of his back, and then slammed him against the wall inside the window. The man cried out, tears streaming down his face. His chest heaving, he breathed heavily between sobs.

Lou yanked one knife from the dead man's neck, wiped both sides of the blade on his pants, and climbed onto the wide sill. "Can I?" she asked, looking at Marcus.

Marcus nodded. His fingers were wrapped around the man's neck as he held him against the wall. The man's eyes were squeezed shut. He bit his lower lip with the three remaining top teeth at the front of his mouth.

Lou reached up and pulled at the knife. "Ooh," she purred. "That's in there *good.*" She wiggled the hilt, forcing the man to cry out, then yanked the blade free.

The man pulled his lame hand to his body and his muscles relaxed. He sighed loudly and whimpered.

"Tell me about Barbas," Marcus said.

The man shook his head, sweat flying from his head. "Uh-uh. He'll kill me."

Marcus loosened his hold on the man's neck and brought the handgun to the soft spot beneath his chin, pushing it upward. "Like I won't?"

"I-I-I don't know anything."

Marcus's nasty smile flattened. He grabbed the man's injured hand and pressed his thumbnail into the open, bleeding wound. "Tell. Me. About. Barbas."

The man winced and suppressed a scream with a prolonged grunt. His eyes were clamped shut and his tears mixed with the profuse sweat streaming from his head, his breathing shallow and quick.

"Okay!" he gasped. "He's in San Angelo."

Marcus raised his eyebrows, asking for more.

"He's at Pearl on the Concho," said the man through ragged breaths. "The old hotel."

"How many men?"

"I don't—"

Marcus dug his thumb into the rip running through the man's palm. He yelped.

Outside the window, Fifty whimpered and licked his chops but sat patiently at Rudy's feet. Rudy frowned disapprovingly at Marcus. Lou was carving something into the windowsill with her knife.

The man puffed his cheeks and exhaled. "Okay. Maybe ten. At least ten. But that doesn't count the coyotes."

Lou stopped playing with her knife. "Coyotes?"

"Smugglers," said the man through his clenched jaw. "Smugglers pick up the women. They take them places."

Rudy's obvious disapproval of Marcus's tactics morphed into sudden interest. He stepped forward, his body tense. "What places?"

Still puffing his cheeks in and out, the man blinked sweat from his eyes and sniffed it into his nose. "I don't know. Places."

Rudy aimed his shotgun at the man's face and clicked off the safety. "What places?"

The man was trembling. His knees weakened and Marcus held him up against the wall. "I don't know," he said. "I ain't never been to none. Honest."

Rudy tilted his head toward the sightless barrel. He closed one eye and steadied his aim.

The man swallowed hard. "Del Rio," he said. "Dallas. Houston. Wichita Falls."

Rudy raised his head and opened his eye. "That it?"

"Some go north of the wall, some go south into Mexico, some go to the big cities," said the man. "Please let me go. Don't kill me."

Marcus released his hold on the man and lowered the weapon from his chin. He took two steps back. He glanced at Rudy and Lou before settling his gaze back on the wounded man.

"What's your name?" he asked.

"Vic."

Marcus patted the man on the chest. "Vic, the good news is I'm not going to kill you."

Vic sighed, his face curling into an ugly cry. His shoulders shuddered and he sank to the floor, his back flat against the wall next to the sill. His eyes avoided looking at his dead compadre's body.

"The bad news is I'm not letting you go," said Marcus.

"What?" asked Lou and Rudy in unison, their faces mirror images of one another.

Marcus nodded at the sniveling Vic. "We're taking him with us. He knows where to go."

"We can't trust him," said Rudy. "Are you kidding, Marcus?"

"If he leads us astray, he'll die right along with us," Marcus replied. "I think he's proven how badly he wants to live. Isn't that right, Vic?"

Vic, holding his wounded hand in the other, nodded.

"We only have three horses," said Lou. "What about that?"

"He's not riding on a horse," said Marcus. "He's walking."

"That'll slow us down," said Rudy. "We need to get to San Angelo. We need to get my wife and cousin's wife back."

"Better we're slow and smart than fast and stupid," said Marcus. "There's a hardware store a block back. I bet we find rope or a chain or something that'll keep him tied to my horse. You keep an eye on him. I'll go take a look."

Without waiting for their protests, Marcus climbed through the window and around the dead man's body. "You mind your manners now, Vic," he said as he handed the handgun to Lou and retraced his steps toward the hardware store.

Marcus wiped his hands on his denim jacket and tugged on the bottom of it to pull it straight. The thing might as well have been a wearable dishrag it had so many stains on it: sweat, dirt, grease, blood.

He and Lola's son, Sawyer, had found it during one of their hunting trips a couple of years earlier. They'd been tracking a herd of whitetail deer from one virtually dry watering hole to another. They'd lost track of it a couple of times, when Sawyer heard the doe bleating.

"I've got an eye on one of them," the boy had said. "It's a buck. It's horning on the lick of that mesquite over there. The doe can't be far from him."

Marcus had looked through the scope of his rifle and had seen the large male deer scraping its antler on a low branch of the tree.

"Before you take the shot," said Marcus, "you gotta answer the trivia."

"Again?" Sawyer had whined.

"You've gotta respect what it is you're about to kill."

Sawyer had smirked. "You respect every person you kill?"

"I respect that they'll kill me first if they get the chance. So tell me, what is the fourth chamber of the whitetail's stomach?"

"Please," Sawyer had said, "challenge me. Abomasum."

"Fire away."

Sawyer had taken a single shot, frightening the birds into flight from their perches high in the dying trees. He hit the deer perfectly, in a line drawn directly up from the back of the front leg, between one-third and one-half of the way up the body. The buck instantly bawled, sounding like a shrieking human, and lurched forward, toppling to the ground.

Sawyer had looked back at Marcus with wide-eyed delight. Marcus slapped the boy on his back, rubbing his hair on his head.

"Great shot. That'll feed us for a while. Let's go get him."

That was when they'd come across a pair of ratty suitcases abandoned in the middle of the field along an overgrown dirt road. One had been larger than the other, but both were zipped shut and secured with small padlocks.

"Should we open them?" Sawyer had asked.

Marcus had grabbed the larger one by the handle and tested its weight. "It's heavy. It's got wheels. So does the smaller one. We'll roll them back and open them at home."

"What about the kill?"

"We'll carry it liked we planned. I'll backpack it. It's not that big a buck. One hundred fifty pounds probably."

After Marcus had beheaded and gutted the buck, he'd used a knife to cut the sinew behind the bone in the backs of the animal's legs. On the front legs, he'd cut at the joints and cracked the bone, cutting between the sinew and the bone. This had left the lower part of the deer's front legs dangling and attached to the upper part only by shreds of skin.

He'd then taken the front hooves and ran them from the inside out through the sliced sinew in the holes in the back legs and drew the broken bones past the holes to create a makeshift peg button, held up the carcass to drain the remaining blood, and he was finished. With the legs of the animal forming the straps, he'd shouldered the buck on his back. Swatting flies away, he'd moved quickly back to the suitcases and the two of them had marched back to their home, conquering heroes.

Lola had been as excited about the suitcases as she'd been about the deer. She'd grown tired of venison and its gamey flavor. Aside from fish, it was about all they could regularly count on for fresh protein.

Javelinas had been nearly extinct in their part of the world and blackbirds didn't taste good. The occasional rattlesnake had provided a nice chicken substitute, but removing the buckshot was a tedious annoyance.

Like Christmas, the family had gathered around the almost ceremonial opening of the cases, and there'd been something for everyone inside, as if a post-apocalyptic nymph had left the luggage in the field just for them.

The smaller of the two bags contained flowery sundresses and loose-fitting tank tops that couldn't have fit Lola better had she picked them from a boutique herself. There was also a pair of black leather boots a size too big. She managed to make them fit with some work.

The smaller bag had also held children's clothes. There were tiny, elastic-waisted jeans and color-coordinated outfits in a rainbow of colors. They were boy's clothes and a little large for Penny, but she could wear them. They provided some semblance of a wardrobe, as she'd all but outgrown hers.

The larger bag had been a bonanza for Sawyer. There were shorts, pants, and shirts that fit him. There was even an unopened six-pack of white athletic socks.

"Somebody kept a fresh pack of socks for eight years?" Sawyer had asked, clutching the package to his chest. "This is like finding gold."

The only thing in the larger case that fit Marcus was the denim jacket. It hung on Sawyer and dwarfed his thin frame. On Marcus, though, it was comfortable. The inside was thinly lined for added warmth. There were pockets at its sides, a hefty collar, and sturdy hammered metal buttons that ran up the front.

Marcus loved the jacket and had worn it almost every day. Lola had washed it once or twice, but he liked the stains and smears.

"They tell a story like a scar," he told her.

As he walked to the hardware store in Bronte, Texas, there were more stories than he cared to remember splashed onto that jacket. He folded the collar down at his neck, his finger grazing across the bandage there, and stepped to the store's entrance.

The facade was painted blood red. A flat awning hung over the wide concrete sidewalk with cased neon lettering that should have spelled "Hardware". Instead, it read "H dwa".

There was a rectangular hole between twin six-pane floor-to-ceiling windows where an air-conditioning unit had once been, remnant strips of insulation hanging from the opening. The windows were open too. The glass that had likely once provided a nice preview of the goods inside was mostly gone. Jagged shards hugged the edges like manmade stalactites and stalagmites.

As with most buildings these days, Marcus couldn't see much inside from the street. The sunlight only traveled so far into the space. The awning only made the lighting worse.

He stood on the sidewalk, listening for any movement inside the store. The faint odor of ammonia wafted from inside, but there was no sound, so he walked past the windows and in through the doorless opening at the center of the building. The strength of the ammonia hit him instantly and he covered his nose and mouth with the crook of his arm. He stepped over debris and glass crunched underfoot as he searched for anything resembling a rope or chain.

Ten years post-Scourge, where every supply was life-or-death, he didn't expect to find exactly what he'd need. He was prepared to improvise. He walked past an aisle marked "Tools". It was empty, as was one designated for nuts, bolts, and screws.

There were animal droppings everywhere, and what little gray light existed within the store revealed one dried splash of urine after another. There were shreds of clothes mixed with leaves and pine needles on one shelf. Some cracked eggshells lay next to them.

Marcus was nearing the back of the store when he noticed an aisle labeled "Yard Supplies". There were no rakes or shovels. Even the spot for trowels was empty. But on the floor, under the endcap, almost hidden by the lowest shelf, there were two small spools of neon orange nylon trimmer line.

"That might work," Marcus mumbled. He pulled the first spool, rolling it into his hand. The second was harder to reach, so he got down onto his knees, his lower back and leg protesting, and reached under the dark shelving unit to pull the spool free and pick it up.

As his fingers gripped the spool, he heard a cry and a hiss from under the shelves. He shuddered, startled by the noise. Before he could move, whatever it was hissed again and Marcus felt a sharp pain on his knuckles. He snatched his hand back, bringing the spool with him. Something launched at his head from the darkness. He covered his face and felt the animal scratch at the back of his head and shoulder before scurrying off.

Marcus turned in the direction of the animal to see a feral cat climb onto a neighboring unit. It arched its back and bared its tiny razor teeth, its eyes glowing as it warned Marcus to steer clear of its territory.

He cursed at the animal and struggled to his feet, then touched the back of his head. It was wet, but there wasn't any blood. The cat relaxed and licked its paw, then rubbed the back of its ear. Marcus stuffed the line into his pockets and made a wide, careful berth around the grumpy cat. His eyes were watering from the ammonia stench by the time he made it to the street. He sucked in a deep breath of dusty, cold air, and coughed it out.

"You okay?" Rudy was standing in the middle of the street in front of the red brick hardware store. "I heard you squeal like a little girl, so I thought—"

"I didn't squeal like a girl."

"Sounded like it."

"It was a cat."

"I heard the cat," Rudy smirked. "It didn't sound like a little girl."

Marcus walked past Rudy and toward the building from where they'd come. "That's sexist, Rudy," he said. "I bet Lou wouldn't appreciate your likening my genuine fear-laced reaction with a little girl."

Rudy followed Marcus along the street. "I doubt Lou would squeal like a little girl."

Marcus glared at Rudy for a moment before smiling widely. He laughed. Rudy laughed too. They were still chuckling when they reached Lou, Fifty, and Vic.

"What's so funny?" asked Lou.

Rudy side-eyed Marcus and then answered, "Nothing, I was just picking on Marcus."

Lou rolled her eyes. "No big triumph there. That's easy pickings."

Marcus pulled a roll of nylon string from his pocket and moved toward his horse. "I'm going to need your knife in a minute, Lou."

"What's that for?"

"Yeah," said Vic. "What's *that* for?" He wasn't sobbing anymore, but he didn't look good. His eyelids had taken on a purplish hue, his skin almost gray. His wounded hand was bandaged now. Lou had cleaned the wound before slapping gauze on both sides of his hand and wrapping it with medical tape.

Marcus acknowledged Vic with a wink but didn't answer him. He opened up the package and started unwinding a healthy length of the orange string.

"That's going to be tough to knot, isn't it?" asked Rudy.

"I'm going to use a trucker's knot," said Marcus. "That'll make it easier."

Once he'd pulled the appropriate length of line, he used Lou's knife to cut it. Then he pulled Vic closer to the horse and began working the trucker's knot. It was actually a series of knots that provided a mechanical advantage other knots couldn't give.

He'd learned it years earlier from a trucker friend of his named Kevin. While Marcus manipulated the string, doubling it over for extra strength, he realized he hadn't thought about Kevin in close to a decade. In the early days of the Scourge, when he'd made a run to Abilene, he'd run into Kevin and they'd talked strategy. Kevin was a prepper too, who'd used his long hauls to listen to audiobooks about survival and preparedness. He'd turned Marcus onto some of the classic fiction and nonfiction that dealt with SHTF and TEOTWAWKI.

"You gotta read Franklin Horton's *Borrowed World*," Kevin had suggested as they stood in the long line at the store. "It's maybe fifteen years old now, but it's got great advice and suggestions about the right tools to have."

Marcus looped one end of the doubled line around Vic's waist. He wondered what had happened to Kevin. There were so many people across whose paths Marcus had come that were now ghosts haunting his memories.

If anybody had made it, Kevin would have been one of them. Marcus shook his mind free of the thought, worked the knot in the middle of the line, and finished his work at the saddle.

"Is that going to hold?" asked Lou.

"It'll hold," said Marcus. "Vic here should hope it holds. Last thing he wants is to die. Right, Vic?"

Vic struggled against the bind that ran around his waist and to his wrists, testing the line. His shoulders drooped and he hung his head. Blood leaked through the gauze on the back of his hand, but he didn't appear to notice it or care.

Marcus unhooked the canteen from his pack and took a couple of steps toward Vic. "Tip your head back and take a drink," he said and held the mouth of the container above Vic's open mouth. "I need you hydrated, so you let me know when you need more water."

He pulled a Twinkie from the bag, pulled apart the plastic wrap, and stuffed the snack into Vic's mouth. Vic devoured the treat and Marcus gave him another pour of water.

"Let's go," he said, and climbed back onto the Appaloosa. "We've got a ways to go and I know Rudy's in a hurry."

Lou and Rudy climbed aboard their respective horses and the group set off. By the end of the day, they'd reach San Angelo and Marcus would be a step closer to the revenge he myopically sought.

CHAPTER 11

OCTOBER 24, 2042, 8:18 PM
SCOURGE +10 YEARS
SAN ANGELO, TEXAS

Marcus slid from his horse, a sharp jab of pain weakening his wounded leg when his feet hit the hard ground. The wind whipped against him, flapping the tips of his jacket collar into his face. It had taken longer than he'd hoped to get to San Angelo. But they were here now. In the dark, they stood in an old park on the riverbank opposite the Pearl on the Concho Hotel. The snaking Concho River and a bridge was all that stood between them and Barbas's lair.

Marcus slid the Springfield from the scabbard and drew it to his shoulder. He adjusted the scope and aimed it toward the large building south of him. Parts of the facade were hidden by the scraggly branches of willows and oaks that populated the steep slopes on either side of the narrow waterway. The arched windows along the front of the building were curved into half-circles at their tops. Soft yellow light flickered from inside most of them. The hipped roof was adorned with several peaks. There was a large peak at the center of the building above the largest of the arched windows. Beneath it was a porte cochère under which a pair of armed guards paced back and forth. A third guard leaned against one of the rectangular columns, drinking from a flask. To the right of the building there was the loud rumble of a generator.

Marcus aimed the scope upward. "I see three men out front," he said. "There are a couple more on the roof, at least from what I can see in the low light. Anything to add, Vic?"

Vic was sitting crossed-legged on the ground, his bound wrists in his lap. It was dark, but Marcus saw the exhaustion on his face.

"C'mon, Vic," said Lou. "You best start telling us what else you know."

"I never worked here," said Vic. "I was only a customer."

The wind blew through Marcus and he could see its chilly effect on the others. All three of them frowned. Their red-tipped noses dripped snot, their eyes half-closed to avoid the drying rush of the cold air.

Rudy took a step toward Vic and looked down at him. He snapped his fingers and chirped a short whistle. Fifty bounded to his side and sat. Rudy said something in Spanish and the dog snarled at Vic. Drool dripped from his jaws, reflecting the thin band of moonlight that offered some visibility.

Vic looked at the dog and swallowed hard. "There's a couple of guys in the main lobby," he said. "And there's a couple in the pool area. They watch the rooms. I mean, that's what I remember."

Rudy put his hand on Fifty's head and the dog relaxed, licking its chops as Rudy rubbed the dog's ears. "Good boy," he said. "Good dog."

"What about Barbas?" asked Marcus. "Where's he?"

Vic eyed the dog as he spoke. "I never saw him. I wasn't there to see *him*."

"You think you can get him out front?"

"If I don't, I'm dead, right?"

Marcus nodded. "Right. All right then, time to execute the plan.

Everybody good with it? You all remember what we discussed on the way?"

"It was my idea," said Lou, "so I think I'm good with it."

"It wasn't entirely your idea," said Marcus.

Rudy nodded. "It kinda was."

"I agree," said Vic. "It was the girl's idea."

"Shut up," said Marcus. "Just stick to the plan."

Lou handed Marcus her knife and he cut Vic free of the bind. The injured gang member rubbed his bruised wrists, wincing. He said something unintelligible underneath a gust of wind and turned to march toward the hotel. When he reached the bridge, Rudy nudged Marcus with his shoulder.

"You think you can trust him?"

Marcus raised his rifle and eyed the scope. "No telling. We're about to find out. Let's be set to move regardless."

Marcus traced Vic's slow movement toward the hotel while Lou and Rudy unloaded their gear and readied their weapons. Rudy had the handgun and shotgun fully loaded. He ran his fingers along the extra ammunition he wore diagonally across his chest in the leather shell belt. Lou had her knives and the Remington.

"He's getting close," Marcus said. "He's got his hands above his head. The three guards at the front have their weapons trained on him."

Lou stepped next to Marcus and looked south across the river while Rudy made sure the horses were secure, tying all three of them to the leg of a concrete picnic table.

The wind was relentless, blowing from the north at Marcus's back. It stung the tops of his ears and chilled the back of his neck despite his raised collar. The branches of the trees that surrounded them creaked, and what leaves remained rustled like a rolling surf crashing ashore.

"They're talking to him," Marcus said above the howl of the wind. "He's on his knees now, right in front of the entry."

"I wish we could hear what he was saying," said Lou. "I'd feel a lot better about this if we could hear him."

"I wish we had a neutron bomb we could drop on the place," Marcus said, then remembered Rudy's wife and cousin's wife were possibly inside. He glanced over his shoulder to apologize, but Rudy was still with the anxious horses and apparently hadn't heard him.

"*He* didn't hear you," said Lou, "but I know what you meant."

Marcus refocused on the scope. One of the guards was searching Vic while the others kept their weapons trained on him.

"If he's doing what we told him," said Marcus, "he's about to get an audience with the big man."

"If he's doing what we told him," said Rudy, standing behind Marcus's shoulder now, "we just have to hope Barbas bites."

The guard frisking Vic finished the job and then disappeared inside the building. One of the other guards helped Vic to his feet but held him at a safe distance. Vic kept his hands above his head, still talking to the men. They weren't responding. Minutes passed. Then the guard who'd gone inside reappeared. With him was a man with a large beard.

"Barbas," Marcus breathed. "Barbas is here. He bit."

"Take your shot," said Lou.

Marcus pressed the butt against his shoulder and exhaled. He tried adjusting his aim for the wind, which was almost straight behind him but would intermittently shift slightly to the southwest. He moved his finger to the trigger, centering his aim on Barbas's wide barrel chest. And then Barbas turned and looked right at him.

Startled, Marcus hesitated. An instant later he pulled the trigger, but it was too late. Barbas had moved and put a bullet in Vic's head with a handgun at point-blank range. As the echo of the single shot reverberated across the river to the park, Marcus fired again. A strong gust of wind swirled around him and across the river. The bullet slammed into the column next to Barbas. Marcus cursed. Barbas and his men immediately disappeared inside the building. Vic's body was facedown on the cement, blood pooling around his head.

"We're blown," he said. "Vic is dead. Barbas and his men are inside."

Lou was wide-eyed. "You missed?"

"Twice," said Marcus. "We've got work to do."

"Plan B?" asked Rudy.

"What's plan B?" Lou asked. "I didn't know we had a plan B."

Marcus reloaded the Springfield, slung his pack onto one shoulder, and started toward the bridge. "You better come up with it fast, Scarecrow," he said without turning around to look at her. "We're not in Kansas anymore."

Marcus moved with purpose, ignoring the ache in his leg and the cold wind that pushed him forward. Lou and Rudy kept pace, as did Fifty. The dog strode alongside his owner and they crossed the bridge together. As soon as they reached the edge of the bridge, Marcus stopped. The wind was making his eyes water.

"Shoot every man you see," he said to the others. "Don't hesitate; don't think about it. Kill them. Otherwise they'll kill you."

"What about Barbas?"

"Kill him too."

"What if we can't find Norma and Trina?" Rudy asked. "What if we can't find them and we've killed everyone? What do we do then?"

"Don't worry, we'll find them."

Rudy nodded, his eyes wide with the worry. Marcus was counseling him against his purpose for being there; to find his wife and Trina. He pumped his shotgun. Lou didn't say anything, only motioned Marcus to the side, put the butt of the rifle to her shoulder, and aimed at the roof.

"Give me a second," she said from the corner of her mouth. She tensed and pulled the trigger, quickly altering her aim to the left and firing again. A third shot followed and she lowered the weapon as two bodies tumbled from the roof and landed on the concrete in front of the hotel.

She smirked. "Two down."

Marcus slung his rifle over his head. He drew the Glock and motioned for the group to move forward. Together the trio inched toward the front of the building. Vic's body was in front of them, his head turned awkwardly to one side and his eyes open. The line burns were evident on his wrists. Marcus hesitated at the body and considered saying a prayer for the dead man, then thought better of it and pushed into the hotel lobby. The three of them fanned out, each of them moving from side to side. It was eerily quiet, especially in contrast to the gusting, howling wind outside.

There were a couple of dimly glowing lightbulbs to one side of the space, casting an off-white glow across the room. The long shadows of chairs and pedestal tables challenged Marcus's ability to see possible threats.

"Where are we going?" Rudy whispered.

"Just stay with me," said Marcus under his breath and led the team to the far left of the room, hugging a long wall that ran from the lobby to a glass-paneled wall at its far end.

There was light and there were moving shadows beyond the glass. That was where they were headed.

Moving forward, Marcus noticed drops of blood on the tile floor, drips that left a trail from the front entrance to the glass panels. Maybe he had hit someone with his first shot. The trail grew thicker the closer it got to the panels. They reached the back of the room and Marcus took a deep breath. His muscles tensed and he raised the Glock with both hands.

"They know we're here," said Lou. "We've lost the element of surprise."

Marcus glared at Lou. She'd warned on multiple occasions that firing from a distance and missing would create bigger problems. He'd ignored her every time. He'd been right until now. Now, though, was what mattered.

"Is there another way inside?" asked Rudy. "Do we have to come in the front?"

Marcus looked at Rudy and then at Lou. They were both right. His bravado could get all of them killed. "You're right," he huffed. "Let's try the back."

Marcus worked backwards, keeping his eye on the glass panels and any emerging threat from behind. There was nothing. They reached the outdoors and the wind slapped Marcus in the face with a cold, violent hand. He blinked back the chill.

Once outside, he led them to the river. It was nearly dry, just a trickle not worthy of being called a creek, let alone a river. Carefully they climbed down the embankment and treaded east along the front of the building until it curved south again around the hotel's side. Marcus climbed up the embankment and, once he reached the top, lay down on his stomach to survey what lay in front of them.

From his vantage point he could see three sides of the building. Directly in front of him, pressed against the hotel, was a trio of generators. The wind made it difficult to tell how many of them were running, but they sounded like the old gasoline-powered generators people would buy for hurricane season. They could power a refrigerator or a few fans overnight, but not a lot more than that.

"Where are they getting gasoline?" Marcus wondered aloud.

"What?" asked Rudy. He'd moved alongside Marcus on the bank.

"Just talking to myself," said Marcus. He scanned the perimeter of the building, and lightning flashed across the sky to their right.

"Did you see that?" asked Lou excitedly. "First time in a long time."

Marcus looked skyward. She was right. It had been a long time. The lightning flashed again, illuminating the thin layer of clouds moving quickly across the inky black sky.

"There's no thunder," said Rudy. "That storm's pretty far off."

"It's coming this way, though," said Marcus. "Those clouds are moving from the north with the wind. It won't be long. Hang here for a second. I have an idea."

Marcus used his elbows to help him gain traction at the top edge of the embankment. His rifle rattled against his back and swung to one side as he climbed to his feet. He pulled the strap over his head and made sure the safety was off.

The three of them neared the generators and the smell of gasoline carried past them in the wind. All three of them were running. And Marcus was right, they were eight-thousand-watt portable generators. From each of them ran large black power cables extending up the wall of the building and into a window about ten feet off the ground. Marcus coughed from a gust of exhaust.

He cleared his throat. "Let's see how you like this," he said, leaned his rifle against the wall, and pulled the cords from each of the generators. "Won't be long now."

He grabbed his rifle and hustled back to the embankment, almost sliding into it like a baseball player stealing second as another bright flash of lightning strobed in the distance. His heart was racing and he was breathing hard.

"You okay, Dorothy?" asked Lou.

"Fine," Marcus snapped. "Get your rifle ready."

Lou spun her Astros cap around so the brim was facing backwards and perched her elbows below the lip of the embankment. Marcus set himself and checked his scope. Both of them were ready to go.

"What do you want me to do?" asked Rudy. "My shotgun isn't gonna do us any good from here."

"Spot for us," said Marcus. "In case we get tunnel vision, we need you telling us where the threats are. Plus, once we open fire, who knows how close they're getting."

"Got it," said Rudy. He scratched Fifty underneath his chin. Fifty's ears turned back and his eyes narrowed with delight. Rudy patted his head and the dog lay prone on the bank like the rest of them, awaiting further instructions.

Another flicker of light to their right carried with it the distant roll of thunder. The storm was getting closer. Judging from the speed of the wind, it wouldn't be long before it was on top of them. Another flash revealed a pair of armed men moving around the side of the building from the rear. Both of them had their heads on swivels.

"Now?" asked Lou.

"Wait a second," said Marcus. "When one of them starts plugging in the cables, shoot the lookout. I'll get the other one."

No sooner Marcus had finished his instructions than the first of the two men turned his back to them and pointed at the disconnected cables on the ground. The second one raised his weapon, scanning his surroundings in a wide arc. When the first one turned his back to the riverbank, Lou took her shot.

She fired at the instant lightning flashed. The round hit the man in his back, right between his shoulder blades, and he fell forward onto one of the generators. When the second man moved toward his fallen comrade, Marcus plugged him with a pair of shots to his chest. He dropped his weapon, clutching at the wounds as he stumbled sideways. He fell onto the ground, hitting his head on the large wheel of the generator close to him.

"How long do we wait for another team to show up?" asked Rudy. He pointed to the northern sky as lightning flickered. The accompanying thunder was louder than before. "I don't think we have a lot of time before the storm hits."

Marcus wiped his runny nose with the back of his hand. It was cold, a storm was coming, they'd lost the element of surprise, and his brilliant generator move had only netted them two more kills. There was no telling, really, how much of a threat remained inside. It could be a half-dozen men, or it could be three or four times that number.

He cursed himself for not being the soldier he'd once been. Major Marcus Battle never would have gotten his team to this point without three or four viable endgames. Then again, he never would have lost his home and his family twice. He never would have been weak enough to fall prey to the seductive darkness of revenge. Marcus bit the inside of his cheek and clenched his jaw. He had to remind himself he wasn't Major Marcus Battle anymore. He hadn't been for a long time. He was a fractured, Frankenstein's monster, a Mr. Hyde version of Marcus Battle.

His gut told him to storm the place, as he had the golf club in Abilene. But with Lou, Rudy, and Fifty at his side, he couldn't risk their lives for the satisfaction of some Rambo-esque attack that left everyone dead.

Thunder boomed closer after a prolonged strobe of lightning and Marcus didn't have to consider options anymore. There was only one, and it was leaving en masse from the rear of the hotel building.

A half dozen or more men were marching across the back parking lot toward a three-level concrete parking garage. He couldn't be sure, but Marcus thought Barbas was among them.

They were maybe two hundred yards away and well within the rifle's range. Marcus had three shots left in the Springfield. He worked the bolt and lowered his eye to the scope.

"You see that?" he asked Lou.

"Already on it," she said. "Ready when you are."

"If they start running, we do too," Marcus said.

"Got it," said Lou. "Say the word."

"Ready," said Rudy.

"In three," Marcus said, setting his aim on his target. "I've got the man in front."

"I've got the back," said Lou.

"Three." Marcus drew his finger to the trigger and exhaled. "Two." He relaxed and focused on the target. "One."

Marcus pulled his trigger and the rifle kicked back into his shoulder. A moment later the man in the front of the group went limp and dropped. Marcus cranked the bolt and aimed at the man right behind the first target. He exhaled and fired. The second man spun around and stumbled backward but didn't fall. Marcus emptied his rifle with the third shot, finishing off the injured man.

With his scope, he could see Lou had dropped two other men. There were three still standing. But they weren't running. They'd turned and were moving toward them.

Marcus pulled another five rounds from his pocket and quickly loaded them into the rifle. A gust of wind carried with it a fine mist. Lightning flickered overhead and thunder cracked almost immediately. Another five men emerged from the rear of the building and joined the three who'd survived the initial volley. They were returning fire now, the muzzle flashes from their weapons strobing. Bullets were zipping past their heads where they ducked, pinging the ground in front of them and to the sides. Rudy ordered Fifty to the bottom of the ravine. The dog obeyed reluctantly and descended the embankment to the trickle of water at the bottom.

Another gust of cold wind and crack of thunder brought with them thick drops of rain, which hit the dry ground like tiny bombs, kicking up the dust into a low haze that looked like dirty fog. Marcus took aim at one of the approaching men and hit him in the leg. The man grabbed at the wound and Marcus drilled him with a second shot. Beside him, he could hear the crack of Lou's rifle. The sounds of gunfire mixed with the increasingly frequent cracks of thunder overhead. A sheet of rain swept across them right to left, engulfing the fight in a downpour.

In the dark, through the shower and dust, Marcus had trouble with the scope, so he abandoned it and lifted his head. He cranked the bolt and unleashed another shot, and another.

"I'm out!" Lou cried over the cacophony of the storm.

Marcus took aim and fired his last round, missing the gangster he intended to kill. He reached into his pocket and grabbed a handful of rounds, quickly reloaded, and handed Lou the rest. The approaching gang was less than a hundred yards away.

Lou wiped the rain from her face and spun her hat so it protected her eyes, sinking her elbows back into what was now a thin layer of mud. She fired a quick couple of rounds, stopping one advancing threat before Rudy called out a warning.

He was pointing toward the river beneath them. "We've got a problem," he said. "The ground can't hold the water."

The land was so dry it wasn't absorbing the torrential downpour quickly enough. It was running off the dirt and down the embankment into the riverbed. What had been a trickle a few minutes earlier was visibly deeper with an aggressive current. Fifty had moved from the bottom of the ravine to halfway up. His ears were back as he carefully watched the water rise.

Marcus looked over his shoulder at the rising river, cursed aloud, and then turned back to face the oncoming attack. A bullet whizzed by him, clipping his jacket on the right shoulder.

Because of the rain, it was hard to focus on the shadows and figures moving toward them at odd angles. He paid attention to muzzle flashes and aimed his fire at them. Twice he stopped the man behind the weapon. Still more men came. It was as if they were descending on them from the clouds.

Lou throttled another attacker with a true shot. "How many are there?" she asked above the din. "This isn't good."

Another shot grazed Marcus's hand and ricocheted off the rifle. He grunted in pain and dropped the weapon into the mud.

Lou looked at him with wide eyes. Lightning flashed, revealing her furrowed brow and downward-curled mouth. "You okay?"

"I'm good," he said. "Just got dinged."

She nodded and went back to business.

Marcus drew his Glock. Some of the men were close enough now it made sense. He pushed himself from the momentary safety of the ravine and rolled through the mud until he could right himself. From one knee he raised the handgun, depressing the trigger safety as he applied pressure. Within seconds he'd unloaded the magazine and taken down four more men. Lightning and thunder cracked and crashed simultaneously, sending a violent shudder through the length of his body.

He reached into his pocket, thinking he'd added an extra loaded magazine there. He hadn't. All he found were the remaining few rounds for the Springfield. His pack was with the horses. This wasn't conduct becoming Major Marcus Battle.

Another flare of lightning lit up Marcus's surroundings. There were at least three men marching in his direction. How they hadn't hit him yet was remarkable. Or divine intervention, or perhaps dumb luck. To his left was the outstretched arm of a dead man, his AK-47 still in his hand.

Marcus rolled to his right and grabbed the weapon, dragging it through the thin slop until he had it in his hands. He was on his back, positioned as if he were halfway through a sit-up. There was no way to get the proper leverage, but he held the rifle tight against his shoulder and sprayed his surroundings, tapping the trigger repeatedly and mowing down the trio closest to him.

Heavy, cold pellets of rain slapped against his face. His clothes were soaked and stuck to his body. His ears were ringing with a high-pitched tone. His mind flashed for a split second to his time in Syria and the close-quarters combat he'd frequently endured.

Marcus rolled over onto his stomach and sank his elbows into the ground. The sounds of gunfire rattled and cracked alongside the thunder that pealed from above, crashing and reverberating around him. The wind blew the rain and the muck onto his cheeks and into his eyes. He settled himself, the rifle positioned in his hands and against his body, and pulled the trigger again, aiming for a bright muzzle flash at his ten o'clock. He fired again at a man running straight at him. The man must not have seen him, though, as he was firing well over Marcus's head. Marcus hit the man twice before he stumbled forward and landed on top of Marcus, sliding into him and knocking the rifle from his hands.

The man, bleeding and grunting, struggled with Marcus and then used his weight to pin him to the ground. He was a large man and easily outweighed Marcus by thirty or forty pounds.

He cursed with a hoarse, scratchy voice and clawed, his thickly calloused hands finding their way to Marcus's face, pressing his face into the muck.

Marcus sucked in a mouthful of glop and tried coughing it out but couldn't. Facedown in the mud, he could feel the man leaning on him, holding him down. Marcus flailed, kicked his feet, and grasped with his hands at nothing. He couldn't breathe. His chest started to burn and his head buzzed. He was losing consciousness.

The man started laughing. Above the noise of the wind, rain, and fighting, Marcus felt the vibration of the man's laughter against his body. Then Marcus heard a loud, trilling whistle and the laughter stopped, the pressure on his back and head instantly gone.

Marcus instantly raised his head and took a ragged, desperate breath. Coughing up the filth in his mouth, he fell onto his side and felt a struggle at his back. His ears were ringing, his vision blurry. The gunfire had ended, but in the distance he could hear screaming and a gnarling growl. Marcus struggled onto his knees and felt something warm and wet slap against the side of his face. He touched the spot and looked at his bloodied hand.

Slowly, as he focused, he understood what had happened. The man's body was on the ground, twitching, his face unrecognizable as human. There were pieces of it strewn about. It was his nose that had hit Marcus on the cheek.

The sting of bile traveled up his throat and Marcus retched. It was as nauseating as anything he'd ever seen, and the architect of it was a four-legged mutt.

Fifty was still tearing at the man's neck when Rudy called him off. The dog looked up at his owner. He wagged his tail and smacked his mouth as if he'd eaten a spoonful of peanut butter.

Lou appeared from the darkness, muddied and drenched, cradling the Remington across her chest. The Astros cap was askew atop her head and her hair hung over her eyes.

Rudy reached out and offered Marcus his hand. Marcus took it and pulled himself to his feet. A prolonged strobe of lightning illuminated the battlefield, revealing the breadth of the massacre.

Somehow Marcus, Rudy, Lou, and Fifty had slain at least twenty men. Their bodies stretched the distance from their position to the rear of the hotel.

"I whistled," said Rudy. "That's the signal for Fifty to attack. I don't tell him who to jump. He knows. He knew to help you, Marcus."

Marcus patted Rudy on the back and thanked him. "Let's regroup and go find Barbas," said Marcus. "We need to get him and rescue Norma and Trina."

"I think we found him," said Lou, her breath visible in the cold.

The rain was letting up. Lightning flickered, but the thunder was distant. The wind was weaker, but the air was much colder. The storm was moving south.

"Where?" asked Marcus.

Lou reached down and picked up what looked like a small pelt. She tossed it at Marcus, who caught it against his chest and raised it up to look at it.

It was a scrap of skin coated with a thick, wiry clump of red hair. Marcus tossed it to the side and knelt down over the man's body. He leaned into the man's bloodied, mangled face and closed his eyes. There was a gurgle, the slightest rattle. Barbas was still alive.

Marcus pushed his hands in the mud next to him and whispered in what was left of Barbas's ear, "I don't know if you can hear me or not, but I still got life left in me."

He looked up at Rudy and Lou. "Let's find the women."

***

The inside of the hotel was unusual. In its center, beyond the glass-panel doors of the lobby, was a large entertainment area with a pool, a putting green, and a dining area. All of it was in disrepair and the pool was empty. But there were empty bottles of liquor and trash strewn about that indicated the space was well used.

Surrounding the entertainment area on all sides were two floors of hotel rooms. The second story was accessible by staircases at each of the four corners of the space. All of the rooms had covered windows and sidelights that prevented anyone on the outside from seeing what might be happening on the inside.

Marcus stood dripping at the glass doors with Rudy to one side and Lou the other. All of them had cleaned the mud off of their weapons and reloaded after Marcus had retrieved his pack. Fifty stood in front of them, his ears pricking. He took a few steps into what amounted to an enclosed concrete courtyard and shook the water from his coat.

"Let's go room by room," Marcus suggested. "I'll take the first floor, and you two take the second."

Lou went to the staircase on the right and Rudy to the left. Marcus scanned the open area and moved to the left. The doors to the rooms that lined the space in a U shape were recessed under the balcony that provided access to upper floors. Marcus shrugged his pack up on his shoulders and adjusted the chest strap. His rifle was slung diagonally across his back. He had the Glock in his right hand. He tried the first door. It was unlocked.

He turned the handle and slowly shouldered open the door past the jamb before slamming it open and moving himself to the side while leveling the Glock at the opening. The room was dark and silent.

He moved to the next two doors, repeating the process. Both were empty.

The fourth room, however, was different. It too was unlocked, but when Marcus slammed open the door, he heard a woman's muted groan. There was dim light in the room from a low-burning candle on a dresser that ran the length of one wall. He could see it from the edge of the door where he stood. He peeked around the corner and called out to the person inside, "Are you okay?"

No response.

"I'm coming in," he said. "I'm armed. I'm not a threat. I want to help."

Marcus stepped into the room. He aimed his weapon at where he imagined the bed would be, his eyes quickly adjusting to the light in the room.

The bed was there. So was a woman. She was bound and gagged.

He moved to the side of the bed, sliding his Glock into the holster so he could pull the thin, crumpled sheet over her body and immediately begin working on the binds at the woman's wrists. Even in the dim light, the bruising on her face was evident. Her eyelids appeared heavy. The woman couldn't keep them open, but tears leaked from the sides while Marcus undid the knot that kept her hands bound together.

The woman flinched and recoiled when he touched her shoulder, trying to move her so he could remove the gag. Her body trembled.

He put his hand on her bare shoulder and said softly, "I'm not going to hurt you. I'm here to help you."

He loosened the rag that cut across her mouth and cheeks and pulled it free. The woman gagged and coughed.

"Who are you?" she rasped.

Marcus helped the woman sit up, insuring the sheet covered her. He sat on the edge of the uncovered mattress and leaned over to untie the woman's legs one at a time.

"I'm Marcus," he said. "My friends and I are looking for two women the Llano River Clan brought here within the last couple of days."

He finished with the first leg and moved to the other. The woman's skin was cold and there was a healthy growth of fine hair along her shins and ankles. Her toenails were long and jagged.

The woman coughed again and sighed, her words carrying with

them a vibrato. "There are others here," she whimpered. "I don't know how many. They come and go. I could hear them sometimes."

Marcus loosened the knot on her second leg and removed the rope. He tossed it to the floor and then looked at the woman. "Where do they take the new ones?"

The woman pulled the sheet up to her chin, her bloodied wrists swollen and bruised. She shook her head, her chin trembling. "I don't know. I never saw them. Sometimes I could hear them. I could hear the men talk about them."

"What's your name?"

"Michelle."

"How long have you been here?"

"I don't know," she said. "Weeks. Maybe a few months?"

"Where are you from, Michelle?"

"Odessa."

Marcus stood from the bed. "Can you walk?"

Michelle shook her head. "Not far."

"All right," Marcus said. "Let's get you up. I'll tighten that sheet around you and we'll get you out into the courtyard area. Okay?"

Michelle blinked her wide, frightened eyes and nodded. She took Marcus's hand and stood as he wrapped the large sheet around her frail, emaciated frame. She draped her arm across his shoulder and he put his hand around her waist, helping her from the room one cautious step at a time. Marcus felt the entirety of her ninety pounds relying on his strength as they found their way to a table and chairs not far from her door.

"I'm going to leave you here," Marcus said. "I need to look for others."

Michelle grabbed his arm, her fingers gripping his jacket. "Don't leave me," she begged. "Don't go. Please."

"I'm not leaving the building," Marcus assured her.

She let go of his jacket and dropped her chin, crossed her arms on her chest, and held her shoulders with her hands. Her body shuddered and she leaned back in the chair.

Marcus offered a weak smile and started toward the next room. And the next. He repeated the same, deliberate process with two more women and sat them next to Michelle. Both of them carried the same waiflike physique and gaunt, vacant stare. They too had no concept of exactly how long they'd been held captive, but they were also from Odessa. None of the women seemed to know each other.

Marcus was going to the next room when he heard Lou calling him. He looked up. She was standing at a railing on the far right side of the second floor.

Although her eyes caught the trio of women sitting at the table, she said nothing about them. "You gotta come up here," she said. "Now."

Marcus limped to the staircase on the right side of the courtyard and pulled himself upward to the balcony. Most of the doors to the second-floor rooms were open.

"So you found some survivors," Lou said, issuing a statement as much as asking a question.

Marcus nodded, his eyes dancing between the open doors and Lou. "Yeah," he said. "You?"

Lou shook her head. "Some of the rooms are empty," she said. "Some of them aren't."

"What do you mean?"

Lou took a deep breath, held it, and exhaled. "I mean the women are dead."

Marcus curled his fists into tight balls. "Where's Rudy?"

Lou motioned toward a room over her shoulder. "He's with Trina."

"She's...?"

"Yeah."

"What about Norma?"

"We haven't found her."

Marcus lowered his head and nodded. "I'm going in there. You can go downstairs and keep the women company if you want."

"Have you finished the rooms downstairs?" she asked.

"There are a few more," Marcus said.

"I'll check them," said Lou. She slid past Marcus to the stairs, bounding down to the first floor.

Marcus clenched his jaw and entered the room where Rudy had found his cousin's wife. He was sitting on the edge of the mattress with his head in his hands. His fingers tugged at his hair and he rocked back and forth. Behind him on the bed was Trina.

Her partially nude body was pale, her eyes fixed open, mouth agape.

"Rudy," Marcus said.

He didn't respond. Marcus moved closer. Rudy was mumbling to himself.

"Rudy."

Rudy looked up, his eyes wide and swollen. The dim light glistened on the streaks of tears running down his face.

Marcus took another step closer to Rudy and knelt. He looked his new friend in the eyes and then reached out to hug him. He wrapped his arms around Rudy's back and pulled the weeping man into his chest.

"I'm so sorry, Rudy," Marcus said. "I'm so sorry."

Rudy's body shook as he sobbed. "I don't understand," he wailed. "How can there be so much cruelty in this world? So much suffering? Too much."

Marcus patted Rudy on the back and gently pulled back. He reached around Rudy and, with his thumb and index finger, closed Trina's eyes. He touched her chin and forcefully closed her mouth then looked at Rudy. "We're going to find Norma," he said. "I'm sure—"

"Rudy! Marcus!" It was Lou, calling from downstairs. "Rudy!"

The men glanced at each other and then quickly moved to the balcony. Marcus leaned over the rail, searching the courtyard below for Lou.

Rudy joined him at the railing. "Lou?" he called excitedly. "What is it?"

"Are you all right?" Marcus asked, sliding along the rail until he reached the stairs. Using the rail for support, he descended the steps quickly, ignoring the stiffness in his leg.

Rudy bounded past him, beating him to the first floor. He sprinted toward the table with the three women, searching for a familiar face.

"Lou?" he called.

"In here," she replied as Marcus reached the ground level. Her voice was coming from an open room underneath the stairs. It was the second to last facing the courtyard on the right side.

Marcus beat Rudy to the doorway. Lou was standing next to the bed. Fifty was already there, sitting obediently with his tail swishing on the floor. There was a woman sitting up on the bare mattress. She was clothed, a bandanna around her neck. There were cut ropes on the floor next to her.

Marcus stood there for a moment before Rudy shoved past him into the room. He slid onto the floor, almost skidding to a halt against the bed as he fell into the woman on the bed and knocked her back onto the mattress.

The two of them held each other and wept. They kissed each other, their lips smacking between cries. Fifty jumped onto the bed, trying to join the celebration. He whimpered and barked at the excitement of it.

Rudy asked the woman, "Are you okay?"

"I'm fine. They didn't touch me."

Marcus looked at Lou and mouthed, "Norma?"

Lou nodded and smiled.

A thick lump formed in Marcus's throat. He swallowed against it, but he couldn't stop the tears from welling in his eyes. He knuckled them from his cheeks and leaned against the doorjamb.

When the adrenaline-fueled emotion of the moment passed, Norma looked at Marcus and Lou, her brow crinkled with confusion.

"Where's Trina?" she asked, searching all three of them for an answer.

Rudy gripped his wife's shoulders. He opened his mouth to speak but didn't say anything. The look on his face must have given away the answer.

Norma's expression drooped and she drew her hands to her face. She shook her head in denial.

"I told her to keep quiet," she said. "I told her not to talk, not to badger them."

Rudy looked to Marcus, his eyes pleading for help. He snapped his fingers and Fifty hopped from the bed to the floor. The dog sidled up next to Lou and she put her hand on his head.

"The men who did this are dead," said Marcus. "You don't have to worry about them anymore. I know it's little consolation, but—"

Norma tensed and pulled away from her husband. "Who are you?" she asked. She looked at Lou. "And you?"

"This is Marcus and Lou," Rudy said. "They helped me find you."

Norma's posture relaxed. She flashed a weak smile and put her hands over her heart. "Thank you. I'm eternally grateful. You say you killed *all* of them?"

Marcus nodded.

"That can't be," she said. "They're not all here. The coyote left hours ago with several women."

Marcus took a step forward. "The coyote?"

"Yes, the smuggler. The man who moves the women around."

"Does he have one eye?" Marcus asked.

Norma's eyes widened. "How did you know?"

Marcus scratched his chin. "His name is Cego. I owe him something. Where did he go?"

"Del Rio."

"Del Rio," said Marcus, scratching the scruff on his chin. "That's a couple of days' ride from here."

"We better get going, then," said Lou.

Chapter 12

OCTOBER 25, 2042, 4:05 AM
SCOURGE +10 YEARS
SAN ANGELO, TEXAS

"You sure the horse can pull the cart?" asked Marcus.

He was standing in the parking lot behind the hotel, his hand on the side of an abandoned landscaping trailer. He and Rudy had emptied it of its trash and rigged traces on either side for the horse to be able to pull it.

"He's pretty strong," said Rudy, patting the thoroughbred's hindquarters. "With Norma on the saddle and Fifty and the three women in the cart, I can walk alongside. We'll be fine."

Lou was on the other side of the cart, playing with the dog. She'd throw a stick and he'd fetch.

Norma was huddled with the other women at the back of the hotel. She'd found them clothing and shoes and appeared to be mothering them. The three young women held hands with one another, but none of them spoke or looked anyone in the eyes.

Marcus measured the setup. "You're taking everyone back to Baird?"

"For now," said Rudy. "We still have supplies there. Ammo, food, water. We'll nurse these girls back to health. Plus, we've got a nice supply of new semiauto rifles given all of the ones we took from cold, dead hands around here."

Marcus chuckled. "All right. I don't know what we're going to find in Del Rio, how long it'll take, or what we'll do afterward…"

Rudy stepped to Marcus and extended his arms for a hug. "We'll see each other again," he said, patting Marcus on the back. "This isn't goodbye."

Marcus returned the affection and exhaled. "I'm glad you've got Norma. She'll keep you in line."

Rudy laughed. He snapped his fingers and whistled Fifty to his side. The dog didn't obey. He sat next to Lou on the other side of the cart. His tongue wagged, as did his tail.

"Fifty," Rudy said, *"venga aqui. Ahora."*

The dog shifted his weight on his front paws but didn't otherwise move. Lou shrugged and suppressed a smirk.

"Come here, Fifty," Rudy called again. He whistled, clapped his hands, snapped his fingers, all to no avail.

The dog barked at him and whimpered.

"How about that?" Rudy said incredulously.

He walked around the back of the cart, his hand dragging across the worn steel tailgate. Fifty watched his master cross the short distance between them yet still didn't move. The dog held his ground, even inching against Lou's leg.

Rudy crouched down, balancing himself on the asphalt with his spread fingers. "Fifff-teeee," he said, dragging out the dog's name as if it had done something mischievous. "Come here, good boy."

The dog pulled one paw up to his face and rubbed it across his nose. Then he lay down and rested his head on Lou's foot.

Rudy rested his elbows on his knees, leaning forward on the balls of his shoes. He called to his dog again, more forcefully.

The dog rolled onto his back and pawed at the air in front of his muzzle. He whimpered.

"I think Fifty wants to go with the girl," said Norma. She'd moved to the side of the cart and was leaning against it, apparently as mesmerized by the dog's behavior as everyone else.

Lou knelt down next to the dog and scratched the broad stretch of fur between its front legs. "It's okay, boy," she said softly. "Go back to your daddy."

Fifty lapped at her arm and rolled onto his side. He shook himself and licked Lou on the face. She nuzzled him before telling him again to leave.

The dog turned and hung his head, moping a few feet to Rudy. Rudy reached out and cradled the dog's massive head in his hands, massaging him behind his ears.

Lou stood up and spun the ball cap on her head, tilted the brim downward, and folded her arms across her chest.

Rudy glanced at Lou, at Norma, and at the dog. He sighed and rubbed Fifty's head. "All right, take Fifty with you, Lou. But he's on loan, okay?"

Lou's face brightened and she opened her arms. She called Fifty and he looked at her over his broad shoulder before bounding toward her. He jumped at her and plopped his thick paws onto her, almost knocking her over.

After calming Fifty down, the two parties made certain they'd added to their food supplies from the hotel and said their goodbyes to head their separate ways. The wind had died, leaving behind a wet chill that cut through Marcus's jacket. The clouds had cleared, leaving a starlit sky. Saturn and Uranus were clearly visible, arcing past their meridian three hours before the sun rose.

Marcus led his Appaloosa west across the river, looking over his shoulder at Rudy heading in the opposite direction. He wondered if he'd ever see the man again. Rudy was a good man, and as Marcus had learned the hard way, there weren't many of them left.

He wrapped the reins around his hand and spurred the horse to run even with Lou and Fifty. He pressed the Springfield snug between his body and the saddle horn. With his free hand he closed the top button on his denim jacket and made sure the collar was up against the back of his neck.

"That was really nice of Rudy to let Fifty come with us," Lou said. The dog's ears pricked at the mention of his name.

"He'll slow us down," Marcus said. "You can't ride as fast with him on your saddle. Plus, he's another mouth to feed."

Lou frowned. "He saved your life, Marcus."

Marcus shrugged. "I guess."

"You could start an argument in an empty house," she said, shaking her head.

"What's that supposed to mean?"

"It means you don't know how to be happy or gracious or none of that," said Lou. "My dad used to say that when I was complaining over blessings."

"Your dad, huh?" asked Marcus. They'd reached Highway 277, which would take them the next one hundred and fifty miles to Del Rio. He guided the horse to the left, turning south onto the highway.

Marcus walked the horse over another bridge. The Concho River raged beneath them, the water from the night's storm rushing high along the banks. He raised his voice above the churn so Lou could hear him. "Tell me about him."

Lou snapped her attention to Marcus. Her eyes were narrow, almost hidden underneath the serious curl of her brow. "My dad?" she asked rhetorically.

"Yeah," Marcus said. "I told you about me and mine. It's your turn to share."

Lou sighed and ran her fingers against the grain of Fifty's back fur. He panted gratefully, smiling at the affection.

"He was my hero," she said. "After the Scourge, when my mom and brother died, he kept me safe."

"I'm sorry about your mom and brother."

Lou shrugged. "Everybody lost somebody. What happened…happened."

"Where were you?"

"We were in Austin," she said. "My dad worked for TxDOT."

"The state transportation department?"

"Yep. He was an IT guy. He kept their systems running. We had a nice house. My mom stayed home to raise me and my brother. He got sick at school, then Mom got it. Kinda like your wife and son."

Marcus scraped his teeth across his upper lip and bit his lower one. He gazed skyward and pictured Sylvia and Wesson looking down on him.

"We burned the bodies," she said. "There wasn't really a good spot to bury them in the backyard and Dad was worried about disease."

"Disease? Worse than the Scourge?"

Lou shook her head. "I don't know. He was worried about animals too. And the smell. It would have to be better though. I've never smelled anything like burning bodies. It's the worst."

Lou lowered her head and raked her fingers on the dog's back and neck. They rode quietly for several minutes. Marcus was alone in his mind and he imagined Lou was in hers. When she finally spoke, her voice was low.

"I can't see my mom's face anymore. I can smell the pyre. I can see her body burning, but I don't remember her face. I couldn't tell you what color eyes she had or how her hug felt. I don't even remember whether her hair was long or short."

There was a faint purple haze along the horizon to their left. Sunrise was eking closer. Marcus pulled a full canteen from his pack and offered it to Lou. She waved him off, declining the drink.

"We stayed at the house for a few months. It might have even been a year. We survived on canned food and bags of rice at first. We had a stockpile of cordwood and a few bags of charcoal we used to cook food or boil our water," she said. "Then we started trapping squirrels and tree rats. Occasionally we'd eat armadillo."

"Armadillo?"

"Tastes like pork."

"Never had it."

"You're not really missing anything," she said. "I'd rather eat squirrel."

Marcus nodded. "I've eaten worse."

"My dad said that. And when we left the neighborhood, I did too."

"Why'd you leave?"

"We didn't have land with an unlimited natural gas supply and a well," Lou said. "It got too dangerous to sit still. Especially once the Cartel got bigger. So we packed up what we could and moved on."

"Where did you go?"

Lou shrugged. "Lots of places. We stayed off major roads and traveled through the woods or ranch land. We tried to cross the wall once. Didn't work out. So we came back south. Water was the hardest thing to find. I remember picking at the cracks on my lips until they bled."

"Your dad sounds resourceful."

Lou smiled. "He was. He always managed to find a way. And then he found the library—that was the best. It had bathrooms and carpet and chairs. It even had some old solar cells on the roof my dad tapped into. We could run the break room refrigerator, microwave, and coffee maker. Plus it was near a pond. So for a while, we were good. Plus my dad used the books to teach me so much. It was paradise. That's what we called it, anyhow."

"Where was it?"

"Killeen," she said. "It was on a college campus."

"And you were by yourselves?"

"Until the Dwellers came."

Marcus pulled on the reins, stopping his horse. A chill ran through his body. "What do you mean, the Dwellers?"

Lou's tone slid from melancholic to bitter. "The Dwellers," she repeated. "The people you helped put in power."

Marcus swallowed hard and looked away from Lou. He cleared his throat and kicked his heels into the horse to get it moving. He didn't say anything to refute her. She was right. He *had* helped to put the Dwellers in control of Texas. He had led the revolt against the Cartel. He was partially responsible for the lawless no-man's-land the region south of the wall had become.

"The Dwellers pushed the Cartel people into the dark corners they hadn't explored," she said. "They were looking for safe havens, places where they could escape the high and mighty Dwellers, who considered themselves judge, jury, and executioner."

"That sounds like something your father said. I can't imagine that's how you saw the world at that age. What were you? Eleven? Twelve?"

Lou sneered. "You can't imagine a lot of things, I'm guessing."

Marcus bit the inside of his cheek, cursing himself for having brought up the subject. He should have known better. He'd noticed her bristle at the mention of the Dwellers days ago.

"I shouldn't have said that." An apologetic voice replaced Lou's nasty one. "You couldn't have known what would happen. You were doing what you thought was the right thing to do. My dad told me about the bad things he'd seen the Cartel do. You were trying to help people."

Those words stung. In his heart, Marcus knew he hadn't helped the Dwellers for the benefit of others. He'd done it to save his own skin. He'd done it to get help crossing the wall. There was nothing selfless or benevolent about it.

"But when you shine a light on a cockroach, it's gonna hide," she said. "And they came running for the library."

"You don't have to tell me the rest," Marcus said.

"It's fine," said Lou. "We held out for a while. We were locked up in the library for weeks. We had the doors barricaded. We stayed quiet and stuck to the dark corners. They crept around but never managed to find us."

"They didn't break into the library?"

"They did," said Lou. They broke a window and rummaged through the place. Somehow we managed to stay hidden. They did find some of our food and took it. We ran out a few days later. Water was pretty much gone too."

"So you had to leave."

"My dad did," she said. "I told him I would go out since I was smaller and quicker than him, but he wouldn't have it. So he snuck out."

Marcus took a swig of water from the canteen and then held it out to Lou. She took it this time and swallowed a long pull. She offered it to Fifty. He sniffed it and then lapped at the canteen's mouth as she tipped water onto his nose. She thanked Marcus and handed back the water. The smile on her face that appeared briefly as she watered the dog was gone again. She looked toward the east, where the purple was giving way to an orange hue that arced along the horizon.

"There were a bunch of them camped out by the pond," Lou recalled. "I was watching through a window. I could see them."

Lou's voice trailed off. Her body swayed on the horse and her fingers ran along Fifty's neck and back. The dog was licking his muzzle, his tongue slapping against his nose and whiskers.

Lou shrank from the confident seventeen-year-old who could pass for twenty-five to the twelve-year-old who watched her father die. Sadness overwhelmed her features like a dense fog washing across a field. She wasn't with Marcus on the road to Del Rio. She was back in Killeen, peering through the window at the bad men. Her eyes twitched and her chin quivered, reliving the worst moments of her young life.

"Seeing my dad die was different than it was with my mom or brother," she said vacantly. "I didn't actually see either of them pass. My dad kept me from seeing their last breaths. With my dad, though, there wasn't anyone to keep me from seeing it. I knew I shouldn't be watching. There was this little tug inside my gut that told me to look away. It told me not to keep my nose pressed to the glass."

Lou pulled her hand to her stomach and curled her hand into a fist, balling some of her shirt inside her grip. "There was also this little voice that wanted me to run outside with my knives and save my dad. That voice was eggin' me on, tellin' me not to be a sissy."

Lou let go of her shirt and rubbed her sweaty hand on her leg. "I was caught in the middle, I guess. I didn't do either. I kinda froze there and watched it happen. I watched them take the squirrels from my dad and surround him. They picked at him and forced him to his knees. Then they killed him with his own gun when he tried to fight back."

Her words hung in the still, frosty air. The only sound was the syncopated clop of the horses' hooves on the asphalt. *Clip-clop. Clip-clop.* The sole noise bridged the uncomfortable silence between Lou's admission and Marcus's apology.

"I didn't mean for those things to happen," Marcus said. "I didn't see the world getting worse than it already was. I should have seen it, but I didn't. I was too consumed with my own survival to think about what my actions might mean to the lives of others."

Lou wiped tears from her eyes and blinked. Their horses were even with each other on the highway. She pulled her shoulders back, raised her chin, and narrowed her eyes.

"Everyone's trying to survive, Marcus," she said. "I could blame you if I wanted to, and if I'm being honest, maybe I do a little bit. But you didn't start the Scourge. You didn't create the Cartel. You didn't tell those men to find the pond outside my paradise and kill my dad."

Marcus heard her, but he wasn't listening. He was envisioning orphaned Lou fending for herself in those early days after her father's death. How had she done it? How had she not curled up into a little ball with her books and stayed hidden until she starved to death?

Instead of hiding like he had done for the better part of a decade, she'd attacked the world. She'd defended herself against the enemy, foraged for grubs, hunted for food, and searched for water. In that moment, he saw Lou differently. She'd earned the right to be a smart-ass, to tell him off when he was wrong, or to offer strategic ideas better than his.

"You're something special," he said to her. "Your dad would be proud of you. I'm sure your mom and brother would be too."

Lou tilted her head to the side with surprise. She fidgeted with the hat on her head and stuttered a thank-you.

"Where did that come from?" she asked after they'd ridden another couple of minutes in relative silence.

Marcus chuckled. "To tell you the truth, I don't know. It just sneaked out of me. But I mean it. You're a survivor, Lou, and I'm lucky to have you with me."

"I wish I had an MP3 recorder," she said with a big toothy grin. "Then I could replay what you said over and over."

"I'm sure you'll remind me regardless," Marcus said.

"I'm sure I will, Dorothy."

Chapter 13

OCTOBER 25, 2042, 4:27 PM
SCOURGE +10 YEARS
ELDORADO, TEXAS

The first time Marcus had heard of El Dorado, Texas, John Wayne was a gunslinger trying to stop a rancher from stealing water. It took place in a fictional town in the 1800s before the *real* Eldorado existed.

Now, a century and a half later, the town that sat a hundred miles from Ciudad Acuña, Mexico, would have been lucky to have water at all. Much of it was a barren wasteland not far from the southern wall that kept Texans from easily migrating into Mexico and vice versa.

The town was a crisscross of streets laid out like a diagonal mesh that ran for a dozen blocks in all directions. The buildings were a mix of modest homes, abandoned businesses, and old government buildings. Some of them were occupied. Faces leered at them through their dust-painted windows. None of them came outside or approached them. That was a good thing. Marcus had one hand wrapped around the Springfield. Lou was gripping a knife at her waist.

The streets were coated in dust and dirt too. Almost all of them lay under layers of sandy brown grime as if nobody had traveled on them for weeks or even months. One street was clean of the silt, though. Divide Street was well traveled. It was the extension of Highway 277 that ran due southwest through the center of town.

Marcus, Lou, and Fifty had reached the edge of town, about to put Eldorado behind them when an elderly man and woman appeared in the parking lot of an old Dollar General. The man waved at them, his hands high above his head. His face was a road map of wrinkles, the loose-sagging skin drooped from jowls like it was hung there to dry. The woman was younger, though not by much. Her white hair was pulled back neatly into a tight bun atop her head. The couple reminded Marcus of a post-apocalyptic *American Gothic*. All that was missing was the three-tined hayfork.

Marcus and Lou slowed their horses to a stop. Marcus raised his weapon, aiming it at the ground in front of the couple's feet. He waited for the man to speak. Fifty lifted his head and whimpered.

"Afternoon, stranger," said the old man, his voice weak and raspy. He stood in place, shifting his weight from foot to foot. He'd put one hand on his wife's shoulder. She stood with her hands clasped neatly in front of her, a grim look on her face.

"Hey," said Marcus.

"We don't see to many strange men make their way through here," the old man said.

Marcus cocked his head to one side. "Strange?"

The man looked at the ground and shook his head. "I ain't so good with words. What I mean to say is most of the people who come through here is women."

"Women?"

"I mean to say, the men we all know. We seen them lots. It's the women we don't know. Plus they don't let 'em have pets like you do."

Lou put her hand on Fifty's thick head and rubbed the loose skin with her palm. Marcus glanced at her and back at the old man.

"I'm confused," Marcus said. "What are you trying to say?"

The wife huffed. "My husband is asking if that girl you got is for sale like the rest of them."

Marcus raised his weapon, aiming it squarely at the woman. Her expression remained flat and unchanged. The old man gripped her shoulder more tightly. Fifty's whimper rolled into a low growl, the hair on the back of his neck and between his shoulders standing on end. Lou calmed him with a whisper.

"If she ain't for sale," said the woman, "just say she ain't for sale. But most of you men, the ones we recognize who come through the Zion Ranch on their way to Del Rio, offer pretty fair prices. We got food and even a well that still works. We could trade a couple gallons of it for a pretty one like her. Plus she looks healthy. She could work real nice in the field."

"Where's Zion Ranch?" asked Lou.

A smile wormed its way slowly across the woman's face. Her thin brows arched. "You let her speak too? You *is* a stranger."

"Where is Zion Ranch?" Marcus asked.

The man shook his head, the loose wattle under his neck flapping. "So you ain't one of them? Townsfolk told us you looked like one of them. That's why we hustled over here to offer you a fair price."

"You're asking if I'm LRC?" Marcus asked.

"Duh," the woman said. "What else you think we're talking about? Sheesh, you're strange and thick."

"You talk tough with a rifle pointed at you," said Lou.

The woman chuckled. "You got too many questions to shoot us dead."

"Where is the ranch?" Marcus pressed.

"Back the way you came," said the man. "Up 77 northeast of here. But I wouldn't go there with that girl. They'll just as soon take her as they will give you anything in exchange. Our price is gonna be better. I'm telling you."

"I'll take my chances," said Marcus.

The woman reached up and removed the old man's hand from her shoulder. He nearly lost his balance, but stayed upright. She pointed an angry finger at the man and snarled at him as if Marcus and Lou weren't feet away. "You shouldn't be giving strangers help. They ain't helping us none. We got no idea if he's working with LRC or against 'em."

The man shrugged and mumbled an apology. The woman huffed and cursed at him. She started marching back toward the side of the Dollar General, where, for the first time, Marcus noticed an old golf cart.

The woman plopped behind the wheel, pulled the choke, and pressed down on the gas pedal. The cart rumbled to life. Fifty's ears pricked. "You coming or not?" she called to the man.

He lowered his head without giving another look at Marcus or Lou, and hobbled to the cart. Rather than driving to meet the man and make his walk easier, she waited for him to grab the frame and slide gingerly into the passenger seat.

The woman punched on the accelerator. The car burped and rumbled past them, the woman glaring at them as they disappeared into town.

Marcus followed them with his weapon until he couldn't see them anymore. He rested it on the saddle.

Lou raised her eyebrows, bemused. "Well, that was weird. I mean creepy weird, right?"

"Yeah," Marcus said, his words drawn out. "It was creepy weird."

"What are you thinking?"

"A couple of things."

"Both of them mean we're heading to the ranch instead of Del Rio, don't they?"

"We're still going to Del Rio," said Marcus.

"But not until after we find out what's going on at that ranch," Lou clarified.

Marcus took a deep breath and exhaled. "Not until we find out what's going on at that ranch."

Chapter 14

OCTOBER 25, 2042, 6:10 PM
SCOURGE +10 YEARS
YEARNING FOR ZION RANCH, TEXAS

It didn't hit Marcus until they reached the outskirts of the ranch. The Zion Ranch was actually the Yearning For Zion Ranch. He'd heard about it, read about it, but hadn't put two and two together.

YFZ was a seventeen-hundred-acre facility northeast of downtown Eldorado, started in 2003 for a fundamentalist religious sect. In a short time they'd built a large temple, a mansion for the sect's then leader, log cabins, concrete houses, a stone quarry, generators, a garden, and grain silos. How they'd lived at the ranch and the government's efforts to stop it made headlines at the time. Marcus had been a young kid then. The stories didn't resonate with him until years later when the ranch was eventually shut down. Now apparently YFZ was a perfect base of operations for the Llano River Clan and their affiliates.

They were a few hundred yards from the ranch's entrance off Highway 77 when Marcus first spotted the white dome and spire of the large stone temple at the compound's center. As they drew closer, they could see the long, low-slung cabins and outbuildings that dotted the acreage between scrub oaks and mesquite.

"Why is it we always end up in a dangerous place at night?" asked Lou. "Really. Every time the sun goes down, we're riding up on some nasty compound. Tell me again why we're here?"

"Something important happens here," Marcus said. "We need to find out what it is and stop it if we can. Plus, if what that creepy couple said about this being a way station is true, it's possible Cego is here."

They were riding east, the low sun at their backs, moving along the southern side of the ranch. The resonant sounds of generators grumbled to their left beyond a fence that ran the length of the dirt road on which they rode. Lou sped up and moved ahead of Marcus a couple of lengths, her attention on the ranch. "I don't see anybody," she called over her shoulder.

"They're here," Marcus said. "I'm sure of it."

At the intersection with a dirt road that led to the heart of the ranch, there was an open gate. They stopped there and Lou helped Fifty from the saddle. The dog sniffed the ground, walked toward some brush, and lifted his leg.

"I guess we go ahead?" asked Lou. "I mean why come this far and stop, right?"

"Right." Marcus spurred his horse north, through the open gate, and Lou followed. She called for Fifty and the dog trotted alongside, his nose alternately in the air and in the dirt.

The rumbling of the generators grew louder, but it was still in the distance. As they rode along, however, Marcus noticed rows of dusty solar panels similar to the ones he'd seen at the Pearl on the Concho. The rain must have missed Eldorado.

"Just because they're evil doesn't mean they're stupid," said Marcus. "They've got a nice setup here."

"My dad used to say, 'If all crooks were smart, cops would never catch anybody,'" said Lou. "There were jails full of stupid before the Scourge."

The farther they moved into the compound, the less they talked and the more focused they became. Marcus scanned the edges of the dirt roads. When they reached a road lined with cabins, he stopped his Appaloosa, tied it off to a fence post, and helped Lou from her saddle.

He grabbed the Springfield with both hands. Lou apparently took her cue and drew her knives from her waistband. She stood beside Marcus, flipping them into the air and catching them like a midway carnie.

"What are you thinking?" she asked.

"I'm thinking you should stop playing with those knives. This is serious. We've got three cabins on either side. They're two story. There are probably people inside watching us right—"

"Who are you?" a voice boomed from behind them.

Marcus took one hand from the Springfield and raised both arms above his shoulders. Slowly, dragging his feet in the dirt, he turned to face the man belonging to the voice.

He was a tall, narrow-shouldered man who already had the drop on them. He stood slightly bent at his waist, both hands wrapped around the grip of a handgun. His high cheekbones and dimpled chin gave the man an almost cartoonish appearance, but he wasn't playing.

Lou turned with Marcus, her shoulder rubbing against his ribs. Her arms hung at her sides, the knives pointed at the ground. Fifty sat next to her with his tongue wagging.

"My name is Marcus. This is Lou."

The man held the gun steady as he barked, "What are you doing here? This is private land."

"We're just looking for shelter," said Marcus. "Maybe some water."

"My dog's awfully thirsty, mister," added Lou for effect.

"You're trespassing," said the man. "Besides, there ain't no water here."

Marcus looked around, his eyes wide and a knowing grin on his face. "Maybe not," he said, "but you do have plenty of shelter."

"You need to drop your weapons," said the man.

"Who are you?" asked Lou. "What's your name? And why are you so inhospitable? It's like you've got something to hide."

The man's eyes twitched. "Drop your weapons."

"Or what?" asked Marcus. "You gonna kill both of us for trespassing?"

A sudden breeze pushed at Marcus's back, lifting the top layer of dirt from the road and blowing it toward the armed man.

The man motioned past Marcus with his big dimpled chin. "If I don't," he said, "*they* will."

Marcus shuffled his feet to one side and looked behind him. There were three men standing in the middle of the wide dirt street about twenty feet from them. Two of them were armed with double-barreled shotguns, one with a semiautomatic rifle.

Marcus turned back to the man and then glanced at Lou. "All right," he said with his hands still held high. "My arms are getting tired anyhow. I'm gonna slowly lower myself to the ground here and put my rifle on the ground. That work?"

"Just do it," said one of the men behind them.

Marcus looked again at Lou and lowered his arms. He kept the rifle extended from his body so as not to appear threatening. "I'm gonna count down from three, okay?"

"Don't make any funny moves," said the dimpled-chin man. His steady aimed wavered, and beads of sweat formed at his brow.

Marcus bent a knee. "Three," he said.

"Put it down," called one of the men.

Marcus eyed Lou and Fifty again. "Two."

Lou smirked and tightened her grip on the knives.

"Sheesh," said the man with the rifle. "Just put down—"

"One."

Lou whistled loudly, a trill of a song that sent Fifty leaping from his seat and toward the men behind them at the same time she expertly flung a knife at the rifleman. It struck him in the arm and he dropped the weapon as a second blade found the dead-center chest of the shotgunner to his left.

By then Fifty had reached the second shotgunner, his weight tackling the man to the ground before the bewildered man could fire a shot.

Simultaneously, in one fluid motion, Marcus rolled over his knee, onto his back, and then popped up with the rifle at his shoulder. With screams of pain and pleas for mercy behind him, he unloaded a round into the chin-man's gut and then his knee.

Lou followed her knife strikes with a sprint to a dropped shotgun and put two load of double aught shot into the rifleman as he struggled with the deep-seated blade in his arm. Fifty growled and chomped, his feet on the still chest of his victim until Lou commanded him to stop.

He licked his chops and leapt to Lou's side. His tail wagged and he graciously accepted a pat on the head. Dark red blood dripped in thick droplets to the dirt beneath his chin.

The chin man was on his back, grunting and moaning. He writhed in pain with one leg bent at an impossible angle, his hand at the wound in his gut. A red stain drenched his thin long-sleeved shirt to the left of his navel. His knee was shattered. His patella had taken a direct hit.

Marcus walked deliberately toward the lone survivor. He worked the bolt and readied another round in the chamber. He stood over the man, his rifle aimed at the dying man's head. He looked back at Lou. "You okay?"

She had her foot on the rifleman's arm, trying to free her knife. She nodded and went back to her grisly work. Marcus sniffed and drew a wad of dust-laden snot into his throat. He sucked it into his mouth and spat it onto the ground next to the chin man's head.

"Where are the others?" Marcus said, scanning his surroundings as he asked.

"No."

"Where are they?"

"We're it," the man wheezed. "The rest of them left."

"What is it you do here?"

The groaning man's eyes were squeezed shut, his teeth pressed together, and he was drooling from the side of his open mouth. Marcus focused on the impossibly deep dimple in the man's chin then poked him with the Springfield.

"I asked you a question."

The man opened his eyes, tears streaming across his temples. "What?" he asked through clenched teeth.

"What do you do here?" Marcus raised his head. He swept the rifle from one side of the street to the other and back. "What is this place?"

"Storage."

"For what?"

The man groaned and coughed. Blood replaced the drool. It was dark, not a promising sign for the man's survival prospects.

Marcus crouched by the man's head and tapped between his eyes with his finger. "What do you store here?"

"Fuel," he said. "Propane. Diesel. Some gasoline. Not much."

"What else?"

The man arched his back. The color was leaching from his face, his breathing shallow and rapid.

Marcus licked his teeth. "All right," he said, indifferent to the man's pain. "I'll make this easier for you. I'll ask yes or no questions. All you have to do is say yes or no."

The man squirmed on his back. He nodded vacantly.

"This place is a way station for women too, isn't it?"

The man nodded.

"Women you steal from their families."

He nodded again.

"Is Cego here?"

The man's breathing slowed.

"Is Cego here?" Marcus asked again.

The man shook his head.

"Was he here with the men who left?"

The man nodded.

"Did he have women with him?"

The man nodded.

"He's on his way to Del Rio?"

A nod.

"You're in pain?"

The man grunted, gurgled, and coughed. Blood bubbled from his mouth.

"You want me to put you out of your misery?"

The man closed his eyes and nodded.

Marcus leaned in and whispered, "Too bad."

He stood up, taking the man's handgun with him, and slung his rifle strap across his chest. He adjusted his jacket and turned his back, walking the short distance to Fifty and Lou, who was tucking her knives into her waistband.

"We need these weapons?" she asked.

"Shotguns don't have the distance or accuracy we need," said Marcus. "You can take the rifle if you want, but we don't have time to search for ammunition. We have another job we need to do before we head south."

"What's that?"

"This is a refueling place," Marcus said. "Somehow they've got supplies of propane, diesel, and gasoline here. Not sure how they came by it."

Lou reached into Marcus's backpack and pulled out a Twinkie. She pulled apart the wrapper and split the dessert into two pieces. She shoved half of it into her mouth and offered the other half to Fifty. He sniffed it and then gobbled it whole, almost taking Lou's hand with it.

"Good boy," she said, rubbed his head between his ears, and

climbed onto her paint. She settled into the saddle and licked her fingers clean of the white sugar snack filling. She left the rifle on the ground, apparently content to stick with her Remington.

Marcus checked the dead men for anything of value. He found a mostly full flask on one and some sunglasses in the pocket of another. It had been a long time since he'd worn sunglasses. They were Ray-Bans. Aviators. He folded them and stuck them inside his denim jacket's interior breast pocket. Then he grabbed the rifle Lou didn't want. He checked the magazine. It was mostly full. There was plenty of ammunition for what he had planned.

"Are we going to blow up stuff?" asked Lou. "That the plan?"

"Sort of. Not exactly," said Marcus. He pulled the pot from his pack and poured some water into it. He offered a drink to both horses and Fifty. The dog lapped up the last of it and Marcus climbed aboard his Appaloosa. His leg was throbbing. He rubbed the back of his neck and twisted his head to ease the tension.

"You okay, Dorothy?" asked Lou. "Or you need to trade in those ruby slippers for some orthopedic soft shoes?"

"What do you know about orthopedic shoes?"

"The library has a medical section," she said. "Have you ever read a book?"

Marcus chuckled. "A few."

The two started moving toward the sound of the generators. The sun sat large and low in the sky and cast an orange glow across the dirt road.

"If you could read one book now, what would it be?" asked Lou.

"I'd love to have a copy of *Robinson Crusoe*."

Marcus scratched the scruff on his chin. "The only one I would read would be a biography about my life," he said. "I'd love to see how some talented writer chooses to describe me. Does he make me a hero, an antihero, a sympathetic martyr? I'm thinking by this part of the story the writer draws me as a saint for putting up with you."

Lou shrugged. "Or maybe the writer makes you out to be a

homicidal lunatic with no moral compass. By this part of the story you're myopically hell-bent on revenge, so much so that you can't see the forest for the trees. You value life so little you'd risk yours and that of everyone around you to accomplish an ultimately pointless mission."

Marcus glared at Lou. "So you think I'm myopic?"

A crooked smile spread across his face and Lou laughed. Fifty barked and wagged his tail, trying to keep pace with the horses as they moved to within sight of the generators.

"Your vocabulary surprises me sometimes," said Marcus. "One minute you sound like you couldn't string two verbs together, the next you're getting philosophical."

"I'm nothing if not full of surprises," said Lou, motioning toward the collection of generators ahead of them at the end of the dirt road. "Same as this place."

There were five of them. Some were connected to large fuel containers, which appeared to feed the generators. There were additional elevated containers attached to tall gravity pumps. Two more generators were set atop wooden wheel carts, apparently set for transport.

"So," said Lou, "not only do they have solar power running this place, but they've also got fuel to spare?"

"I'm guessing they use it to power generators at their various installations," he said. "Everywhere we've gone, they've had them. That bar in Abilene, the golf club, the hotel in San Angelo."

"And whatever other places they use for business."

Marcus hopped from the horse with the new rifle in one hand. He took the reins in the other and walked his Appaloosa to Lou. He handed them to her and pulled the camping pot from his pack.

"You might want to back up," he said. "And take the dog with you."

Lou did as Marcus suggested and moved back along the path a good twenty yards behind him. She whistled for Fifty. The dog trotted happily to her side and sat next to the horse, scratched behind one of his ears, and yawned. Fifty appeared as unfazed by the violence he'd perpetrated as Lou did.

Marcus shouldered the rifle and aimed it one of the elevated fuel tanks. He exhaled and pulled the trigger several times, unleashing a barrage of rounds into the tank. He did the same with each of the five containers.

All of them, with a series of holes in their sides, began leaking. Streams of various fuels puddled on the ground underneath and around the tanks. The odor of petrochemicals filled the air.

Marcus tossed the weapon to the side, picked up the pot, and walked to one of the leaking containers. He held the pot underneath one of the holes as if it were an open spigot. When the pot was full, he walked away from the tank, tipping the pot to leave a thin trail of fuel.

He repeated the process until he'd put a safe distance between the tanks and himself, bent over, and pressed the flint spark torch igniter to the puddle of fuel at his feet. He pinched the igniter until the sparks ignited the gasoline. Slowly, and much less impressively than Marcus had remembered seeing in movies, the trail caught fire. The flames licked at the ground until they reached the collection tanks.

There was no explosion, but rather the rapid expansion of the flames. The tanks had leaked enough to give them a good mix of oxygen to fuel the fires inside. Within minutes, the conflagration was large enough that its radiant heat felt like the August sun beating on Marcus's face.

He watched the flames, mesmerized by their angry dance. Burning what had to be hundreds of gallons of different fuels was spiteful. Marcus knew he gained nothing from it other than the satisfaction of making the LRC's business a bit more difficult to run.

However, in those moot flames, he could see Cego's portly face and the eye patch hat defined it. He could hear his deep voice taunting and mocking him. The words echoed in Marcus's ears as if

Cego were standing next to him.

"It's not turning out to be the kind of day you expected, now is it?" the bandit had said to him as he lay injured in his barn, his family freshly murdered.

Marcus closed his eyes and let the waves of heat wash over him. He balled his hands into fists at his sides, squeezing his fingers into his palms. The tension in his neck tightened and sent a jolt of pain from the base of his skull to a spot between his shoulder blades. He slowly inhaled the heated air and held it in his lungs, listening to the crack and pop of the flames licking skyward.

He exhaled and opened his eyes. Lou was right. He was myopic. He was living for the deaths of others, the men who'd stolen his peace. At that moment, he reconciled that he had no other purpose on Earth. There was nothing else to live for other than to end those who'd wronged him.

Emilio Rasgado had gotten his. Barbas too. Now it was Cego's turn. He would die one way or another.

Marcus turned from the flames, the heat radiating against his neck as he walked back to Lou. She was on the ground, rubbing Fifty's belly. The dog was on his back, his eyes closed. His leg intermittently kicked when Lou hit the right spot. She looked up from the massage when Marcus got close.

"You done?" she asked. "You feel better?"

Marcus rubbed his jaw and cranked his neck to one side. It cracked, relieving some of the pressure. He didn't answer Lou. He grabbed the canteen, guzzled half of it, and then offered it to the girl.

"I'm good," she said, "but you seem…off."

Marcus capped the canteen and hooked it onto his pack. He raised an eyebrow. "Off?"

"More than usual," snarked Lou with a roll of her eyes. "It's like your mood changed."

Marcus climbed onto his horse. "I'm fine. You might want to get the dog onto the saddle. We've got another day's worth of riding."

Lou pouted. "It's late to be on the road, isn't it? Shouldn't we just stay here?"

"No, we're not staying here. We've got another hundred miles or more. We'll ride until midnight; then we'll stop somewhere off the highway. Maybe Sonora. It's another twenty miles from here, close to Interstate 10."

Lou huffed but picked up the dog and helped him onto the horse. He balanced himself on the leather until Lou climbed aboard, found a comfortable spot, and squeezed himself against her lap. She maneuvered the horse toward the south and held it next to Marcus and the Appaloosa.

"You know we're killing ourselves for nothing, right?" she said. "Rushing down to Del Rio isn't going to make a difference."

Marcus slid his boots into the stirrups and urged his horse forward. The farther he rode, the cooler the air became. He was too far from the growing fire to feel it anymore. He looked over his shoulder and noticed the flames had spread to an adjacent cabin. Maybe the whole place would burn. That wouldn't be for nothing.

"Seriously, Marcus," she said. "I'm tired, you're tired, and you've proven your point. You've gotten your revenge. We killed I don't know how many people, we rescued Rudy's wife, we've totally disrupted their business. Why do we have to go to Del Rio?"

Marcus clenched his jaw. "*We* don't have to go, Lou. You can stay. You can ride back to Abilene or San Angelo or cross the wall for all I care. You're the one who said you didn't need anybody."

Lou hurried the pace of the paint to keep up with Marcus. "I'm not saying I don't want to go with you, I'm asking you why *you* have to go? Why do *you* have to get revenge?"

Marcus shook his head. "You wouldn't understand."

Lou bit her lip before speaking. "Wouldn't I? You're not the only one whose family is gone. My dad was murdered. Remember?"

Marcus's eyes softened. "I'm sorry. I didn't—"

"I know about revenge," said Lou. "And I know it is a dish best served cold."

Marcus's brow furrowed with confusion. "How…how do you know?"

Lou's eyes burned with anger and welled with tears, her passion and her pain palpable. "Because I killed every single one of those men who took my dad from me. I waited until they were asleep. I slit their throats. I stabbed them. I…"

Lou's chin trembled and she drew her hands to her mouth. Her back heaved as she wept. Fifty whimpered and then raised his head enough to nuzzle her arms and lick them.

Marcus felt small. Of course she knew how he felt. Of course she'd sought revenge. How could he have not thought she understood, maybe better than anyone, his suffering?

He'd spent less than a month letting his anger consume him. She'd lived with hers for years and valued every sunrise more than the one before it. She'd moved past her anguish, survived on her own, and was now freely helping him pursue his own warped vision quest.

They rode in the purple dark of the new night, not speaking for several miles. When Marcus finally felt comfortable enough to say something, she'd stopped crying and the dog had closed his eyes.

"You dream about it," he said.

Lou wiped her chin. "About what?"

"Your father's death. Or the revenge you took. Maybe both."

"It's the revenge," she said. "It doesn't digest well. It sits there in my gut all the time. Maybe that's why killing people for you doesn't matter to me. I've already got my cross to bear."

Marcus nodded and chewed on the inside of his cheek. She was an enigma, at once folksy and feral, then thoughtful and wise. He knew she didn't need a traveling companion, but he was becoming increasingly convinced he did.

Lou adjusted her hat and brushed the curtain of hair from her eyes. "How do you know about the dreams?"

"I heard you," Marcus said. "The other night. You had a nightmare. I'm putting two and two together just now."

"Just now, huh? Guess you're not even the kind of person who thinks he's smart anymore."

Marcus smirked. "That's fair enough. I sure as heck haven't been smart enough to figure you out."

"There's not much to me, Dorothy," said Lou. "Really, there isn't. I'm just a girl who wants to live the best I can in a world that don't account for people wanting to live the best they can."

Marcus nodded. They had less than a hundred miles to go. Maybe after that there might be a chance to start living again. If a spunky seventeen-year-old with assassin skills could hope to live beyond the revenge she'd sought and achieved, maybe he could too.

Then again, maybe not.

Chapter 15

OCTOBER 27, 2042, 1:10 PM
SCOURGE +10 YEARS
OUTSIDE DEL RIO, TEXAS

The Appaloosa died a mile from Del Rio. It whinnied, staggered, and collapsed on the edge of Highway 277 before it became 377 heading south into town. They were on a bridge south of a rough canyon, having nearly finished the toughest part of the trek so far. Marcus managed to jump from the animal as it fell, bracing himself against the waist-high railing that lined both sides of the two-lane bridge.

There were the remnants of a large body of water beneath them, a former reservoir made from the Rio Grande River, and the highway crossed its easternmost finger. The lake was dry at its steep edges and Marcus considered shoving the horse over the side of the bridge and to the bed below. Lou talked him out of it.

"I ran the poor thing too hard," he said, pulling his belongings free from underneath the weight of the dead beast. "How's your paint?"

Lou shrugged. "Fine. I guess."

Marcus tightened the shoulder straps on his pack. He held the

Springfield with both hands. "I'm going to walk. We don't have far to go. Maybe ten miles."

He walked alongside the paint for the better part of an hour. They were halfway to the center of town, crossing under the overpass for Highway 90, when a pair of men appeared from the shadows. One of them had dollar-sign tattoos on his hands.

Fifty's ears pricked. He growled and tensed. Lou calmed him, holding onto the leather collar around his neck. He whimpered, his body twitching and ready to pounce.

"Where you headed?" asked the man with the tattoos. He had his hand on a holster holding a nine millimeter pistol. The other man had a baseball bat leaning on one shoulder. It was stained with blood on one end.

"South," said Marcus. He kept both hands on the rifle but had it aimed toward the bottom of the overpass.

The man with the bat eyed Lou. "That girl yours?" he asked. He spoke with a lisp from a lack of teeth in the front of his mouth. It took every bit of restraint Marcus had not to mimic him when he responded.

"Depends on who's asking," said Marcus.

The tattooed man looked over at the one with the bat then back at Marcus. "Let's say we're in the transportation and entertainment business."

Marcus smiled. "What a coincidence. So am I."

The man with the bat pulled it from his shoulder and took a step back. He gripped the bat with both hands and swung it as if he was warming up.

The tattooed man smiled. "So you're headed south?"

Marcus nodded curtly. "Yeah."

The man with the bat took another couple of swings. The bat whooshed as it cut through the air underneath the overpass.

"You're gonna need a guide," said the tattooed man. "Or you could give us the girl and we can do the job for you."

"I've got a guide already," said Marcus. "I'm on my way to meet him."

"Is that so?" asked the man with the tattoo. "Who is it?"

Marcus glanced at Lou before he answered. They'd anticipated running into a roadblock before reaching their ultimate destination. This was part of the plan.

"Cego," he said, pointing to his eye, "the dude with one eye. I'm supposed to meet him. He's expecting me."

The man with the bat stopped swinging. The one with the tattoo swallowed hard. Both men's postures weakened, their eyes dancing between Marcus and Lou.

"Cego?" asked the one with the tattoo. "You know Cego?"

"We've met," said Marcus. "We've talked. I know Barbas and Rasgado too. They send their regards."

"We can take you to Cego," said the man with the bat. "He's…on the other side of the border. Is that where you're supposed—"

Marcus dropped the rifle from his shoulder and aimed it at the man with the bat. Fifty jumped from the horse, free of Lou's grasp. He lowered his shoulders and snarled, protecting the ground between the men and his wards.

"Cego didn't say anything about a couple of flunkies taking me across the border," Marcus snapped. Sensing a newfound advantage, he stepped forward, his feet planted shoulder width apart. "How do I know you're not playing me?"

The man with the tattoo held up the back of one hand and pointed to the black ink. "See this? I'm LRC." His eyes were wide and lacking the confidence they'd carried mere moments before.

Marcus aimed at the man with the bat. "How do I know *you're* not playing me?"

The man with the bat opened his mouth, but before he could respond, Marcus drilled a shot right through the gap in his teeth. The man's eyes widened, rolled back in his head, and he hit the ground before the bat did. The shot reverberated loudly in the confines of the space underneath the overpass.

The man with the tattoo started to reach for his gun, but Marcus had already cycled the bolt, loading another round, and had him in his sights. "Don't do it. Raise your hands."

The tattooed man obliged. "Why did you do that? We can take you to Cego."

"*You* can take me to Cego," said Marcus. "And now you know what happens if you don't."

He stepped to the man and withdrew the handgun from the holster. With one hand, he dropped the magazine from the grip, fired the chambered round into the dead man on the ground, then shoved the gun back into the tattooed man's holster.

"Take us where we need to go," he said. "Cego is waiting."

The man lowered his arms and shakily turned around to lead Marcus and Lou south to Del Rio. Fifty walked alongside Marcus. The man was a good ten yards ahead of them when Lou nudged Marcus with her foot.

"Why did you kill that man back there?" she whispered. "You didn't need to do that."

Marcus opened the bolt of his rifle and loaded an extra round. "I didn't like the way he looked at you. He would have been trouble."

Lou sat up straight in the saddle. "Oh. Thanks. I guess."

"We're going to have a tough enough time without some toothless Babe Ruth," Marcus said under his breath.

"Who's Babe Ruth?"

"Really? He's a legendary baseball player."

"Didn't get to the sports section in the library," said Lou. "I was too busy reading Sun Tzu."

"*The Art of War?*"

"*Supreme excellence consists of breaking the enemy's resistance without fighting,*" she said, quoting the Chinese strategist and general.

Marcus had read the book. He remembered many of its teachings. He knew that a leader should lead by example, not force. He'd learned to appear weak when strong and strong when weak. It was excellent advice coming from a general; however, it wasn't always practical, or even possible, in the fog of war.

And Marcus was in the middle of a war. He had been since he'd shipped out for his first tour in Syria decades ago. He was in a war with others. He was in a war with himself. There was no peace for Marcus Battle. There was only the fight.

Nonetheless, he smiled at Lou. "It's good advice. Very good advice."

***

They entered Del Rio a little after three o'clock in the afternoon. There was a southerly wind blowing north, warming the brittle air. Marcus loosened his jacket collar and unbuttoned it, wiping a sheen of sweat from the back of his neck.

Unlike many of the other towns, the streets were narrow and densely packed with buildings, some of them in decent shape, others crumbling. It reminded Marcus of Aleppo but without the constant shelling or the Arabic designations on the street corners and above the shops and restaurants.

He tensed as they entered what amounted to a concrete and steel valley. They were ripe for an ambush.

"Any weird movements or signals and I end you," Marcus warned. "Anything at all, and I pull the trigger."

The tattooed man had slowed his pace. He was walking only a few feet ahead of Marcus and checked over his shoulder every couple of hundred yards. His eyes always found the rifle before he turned back to the road ahead.

They were moving due south toward the old airport. It was an international airport, but that was like calling the House of Pancakes international. They were so close to the border, Marcus could have spit and called the wad an international flight.

"You keeping the girl with you once you cross?" the man asked almost breathlessly. "Or you giving her to Cego? Most people do one or the other."

"That's my business," said Marcus.

"I'm just saying it's no crime either way. We get a lot of folks who can't afford the mouth to feed. They'll give up a young one for food, fuel, or protection. You wouldn't be the only one to do it."

Lou opened her mouth to say something, but Marcus shook his head. She gritted her teeth and scowled.

The man slowed his pace and walked a step ahead of Marcus. He ran his hand across his forehead. He was sweating too. "There's gangs on the other side of the border. I mean, there's gangs everywhere since the Dwellers took over and lost control. I'm sure I ain't tellin' you nothing you don't already know. But I'm letting you know it ain't as easy as it looks to get you to Cego when he's on the other side."

"It is what it is," said Marcus. "Nothing's as easy as it looks."

"You could wait for him here," said the man, scratching the dollar sign on the back of his hand. "We could find a nice spot for you. Maybe even find a girl for you. An even trade, so to speak."

"Not interested."

"You got a bad limp," said the man. "I ain't noticed it before, but it's getting worse. You okay to keep walking?"

Marcus jabbed him with the shotgun. "Just take us where we need to go."

The man was right; Marcus's legs were tired. When they were tired, the muscles weakened and his limp was exaggerated. There wasn't anything he could do about it, and they were too close to the border to stop and rest. Maybe his judgment was exhausted too. He didn't know this man could take him to Cego. He was trusting him every bit as much as the man was trusting Marcus not to put a thirty aught six slug in his back.

Marcus took inventory of his surroundings. He motioned for Lou to follow him and he moved to one side of the street, stepping onto the curb and keeping himself close to the wall of the buildings. It made him less of a target by providing a clear shot to those on only one side of the street.

The tattooed man didn't notice at first and kept marching in the middle of the street. When he did see that Marcus and Lou had moved away from him, he spun around and walked backwards, his eyes roaming the second and third stories of the brick and concrete structures on both sides of the street.

"You worried about an ambush?" the man asked, swinging back around, his back to Marcus. "I wouldn't worry about that. No friend of Cego's should have to worry in Del Rio. But you know that."

There was something about the tattooed man's new tone that had Marcus concerned. A hint of doubt was sprinkled in the way he talked, as if he didn't believe what Marcus had told him.

"Stop," Marcus ordered.

The man kept his back to Marcus. Lou eased the horse to a stop. Fifty stood at the paint's side. He lifted a back leg to scratch his side.

"Where are you taking us exactly?"

"You need a coyote to get you across the border," said the man. "You can't do it on your own. I'm not doing it."

The hair on the back of his neck stood on end. Something was wrong. "Where is the coyote?" Marcus asked.

The man turned around slowly, his hands at his sides. He motioned over his shoulder with his head. "He's a couple of blocks this way. We got a holding room. Everything gets worked out there and then you cross."

Marcus drew his rifle to his shoulder. He narrowed his eyes and held the tattooed man's gaze. The man stared back at him, expressionless. Then his eye twitched and he glanced, for a split second, over Marcus's left shoulder.

"Marcus!" Lou warned, whipping a knife thirty yards into a man about to open fire from an open doorway.

The man grabbed the knife and pulled it from his chest. Blood poured from the open wound and the man dropped as another behind him stepped into the light from the shadow of the doorway.

Marcus immediately swung around, but it was too late. Though Lou had taken out the second would-be gunman with a second expert throw, a sniper perched on the roof of a limestone building next door managed three shots before Marcus returned fire.

The first shot hit the paint in the side, narrowly missing Lou. The horse bucked and squealed. It cried an ear-piercing, high-pitched scream and tossed Lou against a building and to the wide concrete sidewalk that ran along the street, then ran in circles before collapsing in apparent agony.

The second shot exploded into the brick building in front of which Lou had sat a moment before she fell. The debris rained onto her as she pushed herself, dazed, from the ground. She reached for an imaginary knife from her waist but appeared paralyzed as she struggled to maintain her footing and fell back to the ground. Fifty leapt to her side, jumping onto her lap and licking her bleeding forehead.

The third shot whizzed past Marcus to his left, zipping through the spot where he'd stood before spinning around to return fire. He loosely aimed in the direction of the sniper and pulled the Springfield's trigger. The shot missed and Marcus sprinted into the street, finding cover behind the struggling horse.

A fourth sniper shot hit the horse again, silencing its bloodcurdling wails. A fifth missed Marcus, hit the street, and ricocheted harmlessly off to one side. Lou was whimpering behind him, clearly concussed. Marcus fired a true shot skyward. It hit the sniper in the neck and the man dropped his rifle, slumping over the top edge of the building's decorative brick façade.

At that moment another shot whizzed past Marcus, grazing his side. There was a second sniper. He scanned the rooftops. Nothing. He quickly rolled onto his side and moved to scan the windows and doorways across the street as twin shots missed him to his right.

"If these people could shoot, I'd be dead three times over," he muttered.

Another shot cracked and Marcus felt a familiar burn above his hip. He flinched but spun to his left and found the shooter in a second-story window. He thumbed the scope clean and pressed it to his eye, aimed straight for the man's head, and zipped a shot right between his eyes. The man's head snapped back and he disappeared into the building.

Marcus spun immediately back to his right, searching for the tattooed man. He found him pressed against a building on the opposite side of the street. He had his handgun in one hand and was digging around in his boot with the other. He pulled from it a nine-millimeter mag.

"Hey!" Marcus yelled at the man, pushing himself to his feet and marching deliberately toward him with the rifle set for another shot. "Drop it. My finger is on the trigger and I only put it there when I intend to fire."

The tattooed man didn't obey this time. He quickly slammed the mag into the bottom of the weapon and pulled back the slide in a fluid motion.

Marcus followed through on his promise and pulled the trigger, sending a single shot into the man's shoulder. He cried in pain and dropped the pistol Marcus cranked the bolt and stopped two feet from the man's pain-twisted face. He kicked away the handgun and jabbed the rifle at the bleeding hole. The man weakly batted at the barrel with his other hand, but Marcus pressed harder.

"I will obliterate your shoulder if you move a muscle," he said. "Now get up."

The blubbering tattooed man struggled to his feet with his one good arm, using the wall behind him for leverage. His eyes were a mixture of pain, fear, and rage. He held his inked hand over his dead arm, applying pressure to the wound.

Marcus guided him across the street and back to Lou, and ordered him to sit on the sidewalk. The man sank awkwardly to the ground and Marcus checked his own wound. It was a graze at his waist. The bullet had ripped a tear in his side, but he'd be fine. Instead of concerning himself with his latest injury, he turned his attention to the seventeen-year-old.

Her eyes were glassy and her mouth was open. Her brown skin looked ashy. When Marcus talked to her, her brow furrowed as if she was confused by what he was saying.

He put his hand on her shoulder. "Lou, can you understand me?"

Her face brightened and her mouth curled into a smile. "Dad? Is that you?"

A thick knot swelled in Marcus's throat when Lou threw her arms around his neck and squeezed. She was giggling. Or crying. Marcus couldn't tell.

"Dad," she said, her voice muffled with her face buried in his neck, "I'm so glad you're here. I've missed you and I have so much to tell you."

Marcus hesitated at first, but gently placed his hand on the middle of her back and held her. He started to tell her who he was and what had happened, but stopped himself and rubbed her back, comforting her. She rested her weight on him and he wrapped his other hand around the back of her head. Her hat was on the ground next to her.

Fifty lay at her side, his head resting on his paws, tail wagging slowly. His big, sad eyes danced between Lou and Marcus.

Marcus rocked her, as he'd done so many times before with his own children. It was an unconscious parental response he didn't realize he was doing at first. When he recognized it, he stopped for a moment and then began swaying again. Lou was talking to him as if he were her father. She was telling him about the adventures she'd had, the dragons she'd slayed, and how she did everything in hopes he would be proud. She did confess to unnecessary violence but hoped he could understand.

Marcus listened, occasionally mumbling tacit approval of her life choices, all while keeping his eye on the tattooed man. The man was passed out, likely from the pain, and was lying on his side of the sidewalk, blood leaching onto the concrete from the gunshot.

There was no telling how much time had passed when Marcus pulled away from Lou. He placed his hands on either side of her face and held her gaze, forcing her to look at him. At first she smiled. Then recognition took hold and her pleasant expression evaporated. She blinked rapidly and curled her brow in confusion. Her chin trembled.

"Marcus?" she whispered. "When did you get here?"

"Just now," he said.

"Oh."

Marcus brushed wild strands of hair from her face and tucked them behind her ear. When he did, he found a large swelling the size of an egg on the back of her head. That was a good sign. He remembered reading somewhere head injuries were more dangerous without any swelling.

She looked past him, her eyes jittering as she searched their surroundings. "Where are we? What is this place?"

"We're in Del Rio," Marcus replied. "We're here to find a man named Cego."

"Cego," she repeated. "Cego. The man with the red beard?"

"No, that was Barbas. We're looking for the one with the eye patch. Remember?"

Lou pulled back from Marcus. "I don't feel so good," she said. "I need to lie down."

"You can't lie down right now. That's not a good idea. You need to try to stand up if you can."

Marcus tried helping her to her feet. She wobbled and then fell back against the wall. She was in no condition to go anywhere.

"All right," said Marcus, "stay here for a second. We're going to take a break. You'll be able to rest."

Lou leaned against the wall, her backside and the palms of her hands flat against it, and Marcus let go. He walked over to the tattooed man and toed him with his boot until the man opened his eyes. His face was gray.

"You need first aid," Marcus said. "Which of these buildings is a good place for me to save your life?"

The man lifted his head and motioned toward a bright red brick building across the street. From the remnant of a sign that remained in the window, it was apparent the place had once belonged to a veterinarian.

Marcus coaxed the man to his feet, and with Lou's arm over his shoulder, he followed the tattooed man into a dark building with no power. This was not part of the plan.

Chapter 16

OCTOBER 27, 2042, 9:10 PM
SCOURGE +10 YEARS
DEL RIO, TEXAS

The tattooed man was sleeping with a freshly bandaged arm. He was on the floor next to an empty Plexiglas aquarium that still had a layer of decorative green rocks coating its bottom. Lou was not asleep. Despite her protests, Marcus had kept her awake.

She was improving. Her memory was back. She knew where they were, where they'd been, and who they'd killed. She didn't remember the sniper, getting thrown from the horse, or that the animal was dead. Marcus spared her the details of the horse's obvious pain and that he'd used it as a shield to save his own life.

He had also given her a painkiller for her headache, though it hadn't helped.

"How long do we have to stay here?" she asked. "I don't like this place. I'd rather be in Abilene."

"That's saying something."

"Really, though," she pressed. "It's dark and cold in here. When can we finish what we started? And by the way, where are my knives?"

Lou's eyes filled with the sudden realization that her blades were missing. She groped at her waist and searched the dark room, squinting to locate the weapons.

"They're where you left them," Marcus said. "Likely stuck inside or lying next to the pair of men you killed. Those throws probably saved our lives."

She leaned forward, her voice warbling as she said, "I need those knives, Marcus. My dad gave me those knives."

"We'll get them in the morning. Nobody's taking them. And if I hear any noise outside, I'll go check."

"Go get them now," she insisted.

Marcus motioned to the sleeping man. "I'm not leaving you alone in here with him. And you're not doing anything yet. You need rest."

Lou huffed and sank back against the wall behind the examination table. "Fine."

Marcus scratched his chin. His stubble was long enough now that it itched almost constantly. He sighed and leaned against the stainless-steel table on which Lou was resting. Fifty was next to her, his head on her lap. He hadn't left her side since she'd been injured.

"You need a few more hours to heal. You took a real blow to your head. I was worried about you. I *am* worried about you. I can't leave you here alone."

"I've been alone before," she said, absently rubbing the dog's head. "And since when are you worried about anything other than your mission?"

Marcus chuckled. "Maybe I'm not worried about you as much as I need your sick knife throwing skills to keep me alive."

"So you need me?"

Marcus tensed. He'd never told anyone he needed them. Never. Not Sylvia. Not Lola. Not the children.

"Maybe need is a strong word," he said. "But I would miss your wit if you weren't around. You're incorrigible."

"My dad used to say that," said Lou. "He used to call me incorrigible."

"I would have liked your dad," said Marcus.

Lou nodded. "He would have liked you."

They sat there in the quiet for a couple of minutes. Marcus scratched his neck, running his fingernails against the discomfort of his unshaven beard. Lou petted Fifty and nuzzled him. He licked her ears and the side of her neck. She giggled.

"So," she finally said, "what's the plan now?"

Marcus glanced at the tattooed man. He was still asleep and breathing heavily. His brow was heavy with sweat and his shirt was drenched. Marcus figured the man had a fever. Infection would be a problem in the coming days. But for now, the man was fine.

"The plan hasn't changed," Marcus said. "We knew coming into town we'd see some resistance. We did. We survived it. Somehow, and I don't know how, we survived it. It's like these bad guys all get trained at the *Star Wars* Stormtrooper Academy. None of them can shoot straight."

"I liked *Star Wars*," said Lou. "I saw episode fifteen in the theater a couple of months before the Scourge hit."

"I never got to see that one," said Marcus. "Wish I had. Anyhow, the plan is to get this moron over here to take us to Cego. Or he gets another moron to take us to Cego. Either way, we end up face-to-face with the one-eyed man and we kill him before he kills us. It's pretty simple."

"Sounds simple," said Lou. "Now if you could only click your heels together three times and make it happen."

***

The sun was barely above the horizon when Marcus led his motley crew outside onto the streets of Del Rio. Black birds squawked and fought over the remains of the paint to their left as they walked south, closer to the border.

"Give me a minute," Lou said. "I need my knives." She walked along the sidewalk until she reached the dead bodies, swatting away flies when she got close. Fifty bounded along at her side as if they were going for a stroll in the park. The dog was eternally happy, even when it was ripping out the throat of an attacker.

Lou picked up one of the blades from the ground. The other she had to pry from the target's breastbone. She wiped both clean on the back of the man who'd pulled the blade from his chest before realizing his mistake.

She tucked them into her waist and marched back to the waiting men.

"How far is the holding place?" Marcus asked the tattooed man.

"Not far," he answered, his voice weak and scratchy. His injured arm hung loose from his shoulder, his hand dangling as if it were dead weight. "Like I said yesterday, it's only a couple of blocks."

"You said a lot of things yesterday," Marcus snapped.

Marcus's limp was markedly better than it had been the night before. His side ached, and the tension in his neck and back made sudden movement uncomfortable, but he was as good as he'd been in days.

Lou seemed more focused. Her eyes were brighter and she spoke in the quick, short cadence to which Marcus had become accustomed. She wasn't slurring her speech or drawling with a thickly Southern twang as she had after her fall. She carried the loaded Remington slung across her back.

The tattooed man trudged forward, leading them toward the holding room. He moved slowly, almost haltingly, as if he were trying to count each step but kept losing track of the number.

Marcus had his pack strapped onto his back and the Springfield in his hands at waist level. He held it like a protective father might threaten a would-be suitor with a shotgun and he had it aimed at the man's back. He didn't want to kill the man. Not yet. He needed him for the moment. But if the man made any weird moves or gestures, Marcus was determined to pull the trigger without thinking about it and send a shot directly into his spine.

The man pointed to the right a few feet in front of him. "We're going to turn there," he said. "That's the street."

Marcus, Lou, and Fifty followed him onto the street, which was more like an alley. It was narrow, bordering on claustrophobic, lined with multistory buildings that crowded the low curbs on either side.

The man stopped halfway along the street and faced left. He motioned to a wide, faded mahogany door. "That's it."

"What's next?" Marcus asked.

"There's a knock," he said. "It's a code so rival gangs don't—"

Marcus motioned to the door with the Springfield. "I don't care what it's for. Do what you need to do to get us inside."

A smile snaked its way across the man's face from cheek to cheek. "You don't know what you're asking me to do. You're signing your own death warrant. You got lucky yesterday."

Marcus motioned again toward the door with the rifle.

The tattooed man shook his head and spat onto the ground at his feet. He tugged at his collar and winced when his fingers got close to his injured shoulder.

"Cego is going to kill you," he said through his teeth. "I don't know who you *really* are, but I know you ain't friends. I could see that the second we laid eyes on you coming into town. I seen too many of you vigilante types."

"Have you?" Marcus asked nonchalantly.

"So many I can smell it on you," he sneered. "You got this sweet odor about you, all high and mighty, all full of gumption and swag. It always ends the same though."

"How's that?"

The man lowered his voice and leaned toward Marcus. His eyes narrowed and his chest puffed. "When you get face-to-face with the man, he's not gonna take pity on you. He's gonna straight up murder you and that girl of yours."

Lou didn't miss a beat. "And my little dog too?"

"Open the door," said Marcus. "Do it now."

"Suit yourself," said the tattooed man. He swung his weight toward the door and stepped to it. He raised his fist and knocked on the wood in a pattern that resembled "Shave and a Haircut" but more complex. He finished the knock and stepped back from the door.

Thirty seconds passed. Then a minute.

"You do it right?" asked Marcus when nothing happened, well aware the man could have rapped some coded knock that warned the people inside, and he knew that whatever awaited them inside was likely not the coyote promised them.

"Yeah."

"Try it again."

The man hesitated but repeated the odd combination of knocks. This time a voice inside the room responded, "Who is it?"

"Bingo," said the tattooed man.

Lou snickered. "Bingo? What is it with these names? Battle? Bingo? It's like someone ran Cormac McCarthy through a cliché machine."

Bingo sneered at her. Marcus ignored her.

The voice responded, "Who's with you?"

"I got a man, a girl, and a dog."

"I can see them through the peephole, Bingo," said the voice. "Who are they?"

"They need some help across the border."

"Can they pay?"

Bingo looked at Marcus. "Can you pay?"

"I've got bags of marijuana. It's dried and uncut," Marcus answered. "How many bags will it cost?"

"How many you got?" asked Bingo.

Marcus stared at Bingo, expressionless. He motioned toward the door.

"They can pay," said Bingo.

From behind the door, a series of clicks and slides signaled the unlocking of a series of deadbolts and chains. When the handle turned and the door drew inward, a surprisingly short man was standing at the entrance. His face was wide and flat, his nose was broad, and his dark eyes were hidden underneath heavy lids. Patches of mangy black hair decorated his jawline and above his lip. He was unarmed.

His eyes bounced from one person to the next and settled on Fifty. He waved a thick sausage of a finger at the mutt. "No dogs in here."

Lou put her hand on Fifty's head. "He comes with me."

"No, he doesn't," the short man said.

Lou looked at Marcus pleadingly. "If he doesn't go, I'm not going."

The short man chuckled and answered for Marcus. "Then I guess you're staying out here. I don't like dogs."

"You can stay with the dog," said Marcus. "Bingo, how long will we be waiting in there?"

Fifty yawned.

"Not long at all, I suspect," said Bingo, exchanging glances with the short man.

"Nope," said the short man, "not long. You gotta leave that rifle here and empty that piece you got on your hip."

Marcus looked past the short man and through the opening behind him into the holding room. It was too dark for him to see much past the entrance. There was a dim yellow light, the odor of fried animal fat, and the faint hum of a generator. Something was off.

"You'll get 'em back once we reach a deal and you're on your way south," said the short man. "No dogs and no guns in the room."

Marcus looked over his shoulder, up one end of the alleyway and down the other. There was nobody in sight. There was nothing but the distant hum of the generator coming from somewhere inside the holding room.

The whole town of Del Rio seemed like a setup, as if it were a front for something. "What do we do in there while we wait for the coyote?" he asked. "Why can't we wait out here?"

The short man shrugged. "We do business in there. You pay up; we finalize the arrangements. We don't do that out here."

"Fine," said Marcus. "Let's do some business."

"Marcus..." Lou's eyes were narrowed with confusion, even fear maybe. She sensed what Marcus did.

He winked at her. "I'll be good. See you in a minute."

Marcus handed Lou the rifle and dropped the mag from the Glock. She stuffed it in her pocket.

The short man stepped to the side and guided Marcus into the room. He and Bingo followed him inside and shut the door behind him. Marcus's eyes adjusted to the light. He waited for the men to pass him.

"You lead," he said.

The room was mostly empty. There were a couple of tables with chairs, a folding cot in the corner. Frayed extension cords snaked across the wood floor. The short man led them past the room and through another doorway into a smaller room as if he were following the path of the cords.

The smaller room had a hole in the wall, likely a spot that once held an air conditioner, through which the extension cords ran. The rumble from the generator was loudest here and Marcus crinkled his nose at the exhaust as they marched past it and into a narrow hallway that led to a set of stairs.

The short man grabbed the metal pipe of a handrail and started climbing upward, the steps creaking under his weight. Bingo was right behind him. Marcus put his hand on the Glock at his hip, making sure the holster was unsnapped.

"How many rooms are in this holding room?" Marcus asked. There was a single chain of orange extension cords looped around the handle to the left.

"We're almost there," said the short man, his words echoing down the stairwell and disappearing into the rumble of the generator behind them. "The coyote is already here. He must have slipped in through the back."

They reached the landing on the second floor and the short man turned right. Marcus joined them and stepped across the cord that curled its way to an open space on the second floor above the large mahogany door through which they'd originally entered.

There were three men standing there. The one in the middle had his back turned to Marcus. The other two were armed, stopping Marcus cold under the stained wood transom that separated the landing from the open room. It was five against one.

Bingo smiled at Marcus. "I'll be taking that bag of yours," he said and pulled the pack from Marcus's shoulders. He set it on the floor and knelt down to unzip it. The short man helped him rifle through it until they freed the bags of marijuana.

"You gonna take that gun?" asked one of the armed men.

"It's empty," said Bingo. "There's nothing in it."

Marcus wrapped his hand around the grip. "I'm not giving you my gun."

The large man with his back to the room held up a hand and waved off the armed guards. "I hear you've been looking for me," he said with a deep voice that Marcus immediately recognized.

Marcus said nothing. There was nothing to say. His mind, however, started working. He'd calculated a thousand different ways this could go, a thousand different ways he could pull an ace from his sleeve.

Cego turned around, his girth hanging over his belt, his thick hands folded under his arms. "Folks up in Abilene say you laid down the gauntlet," he said. "Said you was calling us out by name."

Marcus eyed Cego, studying the lines and deep creases in his face. He remembered all of them distinctly as the one-eyed man had stood over him in the barn a month before. In his memory, he could smell the man's fetid breath, the rank and sour stench emanating from his body.

Cego unfolded his arms and cracked the swollen knuckles of one hand with the other. He ran his tongue along the front of his teeth. "I've got to give you some credit, Marcus Battle," he said. "I thought we killed you, left you a sure goner after we had some fun with the rest of your family. But you lived. You healed up nice but kept that fire in your belly. You're a fighter."

Marcus took in his surroundings. Behind Cego was an open window. It was small, but let in enough natural light to backlight his features and drown him in shadow.

To one side of the room was a worn, oversized chair with a side table and a lamp. The lamp was plugged into one of the extension cords that fanned out like tentacles from the single orange line that ran up the stairs. Another of the cords stretched to the opposite side of the room, where there was a square table with four chairs. There was a deck of cards, some plastic chips, and some beer steins on the rickety piece of furniture. One of the table legs looked as if it were about to break off with the slightest tug.

Cego motioned to Marcus as he spoke to the other four men on his side. "This one here then commits some more carnage in Abilene," he said. "Those drugs don't belong to him. They were Rasgado's."

Marcus eyed the armed men. Both of them carried semiautomatic rifles that looked like late twentieth-century Kalashnikovs. Neither of them had their fingers on the triggers. They were both standing with their shoulders hunched and their feet shoulder width apart, standing guard but not ready to fire.

Cego took a step to one side of the window, his features reappearing. "Then he meanders over to our good friends in San Angelo and steals girls from Barbas. And he kills everyone he finds. If I didn't know any better, Marcus Battle, I'd say you were the one everyone should fear. Not us."

Bingo stood close to Marcus on his left. The short man had moved closer to Cego and the guards. Marcus breathed in and out slowly through his nose, his mind working over the possibilities and probabilities.

"I could kill you right here, right now," said Cego. "It could be quick like and nobody would ever see you again." The one-eyed man stepped closer to Marcus. He lowered his voice, its depth resonating so low it sounded almost like the generator downstairs and outside. "That's not what I'm going to do though. That would be too easy and it wouldn't serve much purpose. If that's what I wanted to do, I'd have had Ringo here kill you at the underpass."

"It's Bingo, sir," said the tattooed man.

"Bingo?" asked Cego. "What kind of name is Bingo? Ringo was bad enough."

Bingo looked at his feet and mumbled, "At least it's not *Battle*."

Cego rolled his eye. "I digress. Sorry about that, Marcus. I know you're on pins and needles about what comes next."

Cego pulled on his waistband, inching his pants up on his hips. He stepped closer still to Marcus.

"I need people to see what happens to an instigator, a troublemaker, a ne'er-do-well. Understood?" he asked rhetorically. "Frankly, I'm surprised you put yourself in this situation. I figured you were too smart to walk in here all stupid-like. But since you did, we're gonna make a fine example out of—"

A dog's bark sounded from outside. It was angry and constant. Fifty was agitated.

"Shut that dog up," Cego said to one of his armed men.

The guard obeyed and moved quickly to the window. He took aim. But he never fired a shot.

As Fifty barked, and the room's attention had turned from him for that split second, Marcus pulled his Glock and leveled it at the guard at the window. He pulled the trigger and released the chambered round, firing it into the side of the would-be dog-killer's head. The man fell into the wall and then forward, dropping his rifle, which slid underneath the rickety table.

The percussion of Marcus's single shot momentarily stunned Bingo, who was closest to Marcus. He swung the Glock outward and hit Bingo in the forehead with all of his force.

Bingo fell to the floor and Marcus dove to his right, kicking the loose leg from the table as he slid. The table fell and Marcus took cover behind it, grabbing the semiautomatic rifle as a knife zipped through the air from the stairwell and plunged deep into the short man's back, dropping him to the floor.

A second blade found the other guard's neck, and as he fell, he sprayed his weapon indiscriminately, peppering the room and the table behind which Marcus was hiding. Marcus shouldered the rifle and popped up from behind the table to take a clean shot at Cego. Instead he pulled his finger from the trigger.

Cego had his gun aimed at Lou. She had the Remington in one hand, but hadn't been fast enough to lift it into position. Bingo was on the floor, somehow holding the second rifle. It too was aimed at Lou. She stood motionless, her eyes dancing between the two weapons. Outside, the barking had stopped.

"Looks like we got ourselves a standoff," said Cego. "You shoot me and my friend here shoots your girl. You shoot him and I shoot the girl. Either way, she's dead and you live, but you lose."

Marcus slid his finger to the trigger. Was he fast enough to take out both before either fired a shot? He'd done it before. He'd also failed before.

"Then again," said Cego, "we could let her go and you could drop your weapon. She lives and *you* die."

Marcus kept the weapon trained on Cego, his eyes drifting to Lou. Her defiant scowl told him what she wanted him to do. She wanted him to take the shot. She wanted him to finish what he'd set out to do. He tilted his head toward the weapon and pressed it tightly against his shoulder. Two quick pulls. That was all it would take. At least he'd get Cego. Maybe, with luck, he could hit Bingo before he could get off a shot. He didn't look comfortable with the rifle in his hands. Marcus eased his finger to the trigger. He resolved in that instant he could do it. But he didn't. He exhaled and spoke his first words since entering the room with Cego.

"Let her go," he said. "She's out of the building, we count to ten, and then I drop the gun."

Cego nodded. "Go on, little girl. Git. I'm gonna trust, Marcus, your obvious desire to stay alive is gonna keep you from killing one of us before the other of us kills you."

Lou stood there, no expression on her face. She wasn't moving. She wasn't leaving.

"Go," said Marcus, his eyes still trained on Cego. "Now."

"Do as he says," mocked Cego. "And leave that Remington while you're at it."

Lou's eyes pleaded with Marcus.

"Go," Marcus said, "Or I'll kill you myself."

Lou huffed and dropped the rifle to the floor, slowly backing out of the room. Bingo and Cego took aim at Marcus. They had the upper hand now.

Lou's feet pounded the steps as she descended the staircase. Marcus heard the mahogany door creak open and then slam shut.

"Ten," said Cego, "nine, eight, seven, six—"

Marcus kept his weapon trained on Cego. He could take a shot. Bingo probably wouldn't hit him. And if he did, so what? So what if he died here in Del Rio? At least he'd have avenged Lola and Sawyer and poor little Penny.

"—five, four—"

Marcus closed his eyes and pictured his family members in his mind. All of them. One at a time, their faces flashed before him. This was it. He slowly slid his finger onto the trigger.

"—three, two—"

A scream and a growl pulled Marcus from his momentary Zen. He opened his eyes. Fifty was on top of Bingo. Cego had altered his aim and had it squarely on the dog.

Marcus pulled the trigger, unleashing a volley of bullets at Cego. Some of them hit; some of them missed. As Bingo cried out in pain, his legs kicking and his arms flailing under the weight and violence of the dog, Cego staggered back and dropped to the floor.

Marcus stood from behind the table and crossed the room. He kicked Cego's weapon away from his body and knelt down in front of the dying man. He looked in Cego's one good eye, which was fluttering and working to maintain its focus, and pulled the patch from the other.

Underneath the patch was a mangled, scarred mess of skin and oozing pus. The skin around the socket was red and swollen. Marcus stared at it for a moment and then grabbed Cego by the jaw. He tried to ignore the sounds of Bingo gargling and whimpering behind him as he lost his fight with Fifty. The sound of tearing flesh was too much, but Fifty was a good dog.

"Do you know what you said to me?" he asked Cego. "Do you remember?"

Cego, whose body was riddled with a half-dozen shots, shook his head. Tears streamed from his good eye.

"You said, 'It's not turning out to be the kind of day you expected, now is it?'" said Marcus. "I remember it. And I'll remember it tomorrow when I wake up and you don't."

"Marcus!" Lou called from the landing outside the room. "Are you okay?"

Still crouched in front of Cego, Marcus glanced back at Lou. "I'm good. You?"

"I'm fine," she said. She walked over and stood next to Marcus, looking down at Cego. "He's fat. How does someone stay fat when there's nothing to eat?"

Marcus chuckled. "Good question," he said and stood up. He felt light-headed. He lost his balance and stumbled backward onto the floor. He crashed into the table and rolled onto his back.

Suddenly he felt nauseated and short of breath. His neck hurt, his side ached, there was a burning in his gut. "Lou?" he called as his vision blurred. "Lou?"

"Marcus," she said, her voice trembling, "you're bleeding. You've been hit."

He felt Lou's hands on his jacket and then a jabbing pain at his side. The adrenaline was gone, replaced by shock.

As he slipped toward unconsciousness, he could hear Lou trying to keep him awake. And in the distance, he could hear Cego laughing at him.

CHAPTER 17

SEPTEMBER 29, 2042, NOON
SCOURGE +10 YEARS
EAST OF RISING STAR, TEXAS

It was Lola's last full day alive. She was standing in the doorway of the barn, looking to her right. Sawyer was teaching Penny how to use a slingshot. He wasn't having much luck.

She was leaning on the doorjamb. She smiled and then took a deep breath, closing her eyes to relish the moment. She scanned the gently waving knee-high grass and weeds, lost for a moment in the hypnotic undulation. For the first time in as long as she could remember, she had hope for the future.

With every day that passed, that warm feeling of optimism grew within her. Long gone were the early post-Scourge days of running and eking out an existence. Gone too were the dark times during which she did whatever she had to do to provide for Sawyer and herself.

She had Marcus now. She truly had him. He'd softened. He'd become a father to her son and to the child they'd essentially adopted. He'd taught Sawyer how to shoot, hunt, and gather. Soon he'd begin teaching Penny. And for the first time, she had him talking about rebuilding the main house that had burned five years earlier.

Her heart fluttered. It was almost too good to be true.

Sure, while there were the occasional intrusions from the highway, the violence was less frequent with each passing month. Marcus always handled whatever wandered their way. She rubbed her arms with her hands and cleared her throat.

"Time to come in for lunch," she said. "Bring your sister in and get washed up."

"What is it?" asked Sawyer. "Not venison, is it?"

"We'd be lucky to have it, son," she said. "But no, it's just soup. Where's Marcus?"

"He's out by the road."

Lola stepped from the doorway and into the grass. The kids brushed past her as they hustled into the barn they called home. The air was unseasonably warm. She pulled her hair from her neck and wrapped it into a messy bun on the top of her head.

When she passed the treehouse, she ran her hand along the strong trunk that held the structure safely in the branches above. The wispy grass and weeds whipped at her legs as she strode closer to the road. A trio of birds circled above, riding the current past the tree line to her right. They drew her eyes toward the sky. In the distance there were thick rolling clouds. She followed them along the horizon.

"Marcus!" Lola called. "Lunch!"

Marcus was near the road, where Sawyer had said he'd be. He was working on the fence, twisting the damaged wire with pliers. He waved at her with one gloved hand but kept working.

She rolled her eyes. "You're ignoring me."

Marcus stretched, arching his back. "I'm just trying to finish," he said. "I've got only one or two more."

Lola reached the fence a few feet from Marcus and leaned on it. She looked both ways along the highway and adjusted her bun.

"It's warm today," she said. "Maybe it means we'll get a storm."

"We need the rain," Marcus said, crossing the short distance between him and Lola, leaning in to kiss her forehead. "You're sweaty."

"So are you." She giggled. "You work too hard."

"Please," said Marcus, "somebody has to work."

The demure smile disappeared. "You think you're funny."

"I am," said Marcus. He slid one leg over the wooden beam at the top of the waist-high fence and then climbed over with the other. "You know we could use the rain. We need a storm."

Marcus took off his gloves and held them with his right hand. With his left, he took Lola's hand and laced his fingers between hers. They walked slowly back toward the barn, swinging their arms like teenagers.

"What's for lunch?" he asked. "I hope it's not venison."

Lola laughed. She drew Marcus's hand to her chest and playfully slapped it. "You and Sawyer both, he said the same thing."

"Smart boy."

"We haven't had venison in three days," she said. "I try to mix it up as best I can. Unfortunately our master gardener has been busy mending fences."

"So what are we having?"

"Soup."

"Hot or cold."

"Hot."

"On a warm day?"

"I didn't think it'd be this warm today," she said. "It's unusual."

"You know what else is unusual?" Marcus asked as they reached the treehouse.

"What?"

"I saw some riders today," he said, his brow furrowed. "Five or six of them. They were off in the distance. I don't think they saw me."

Lola squeezed his hand. "Should we be worried?"

"No. We haven't had a serious threat in more than two years."

"We should be ready though," Lola said, her tone serious.

"Sure," said Marcus. "I'll keep watch tonight. After sunup, I'll go tend to that garden someone has been hounding me about. Sawyer can take watch."

"You think that's a good idea?"

Marcus held her face in his hands. "He's old enough," Marcus said. "Plus, if somebody's coming for us, it'll be in the middle of the night or at dawn."

Lola smiled, her worried eyes relaxing. She touched his hands with hers. "Okay. I trust your judgment."

Marcus drew her lips to his and kissed her softly. She wrapped her arms around his back and pulled him close. Her hair came loose from the bun and dropped into their faces.

"Really?" said Sawyer. He was standing a few feet from them. "Is that necessary?"

Marcus raised an eyebrow. "Shouldn't you be with Penny?"

Sawyer nodded toward the barn. "She's eating. I scooped a bowl full for her. I was waiting on the two of you. Didn't want to be rude."

Lola patted Marcus on his chest. "Guess we're raising him right. He'll make a woman very happy someday."

She backed away from Marcus and sidled next to Sawyer. She put her hand on his head and tousled his hair. "Such a good boy."

Sawyer rolled his eyes. "Can we go eat, please? I'm hungry."

Marcus scratched his chin and moved toward the barn, leading Lola and Sawyer to lunch. "Me too."

Lola followed her men inside. She paused at the barn door and looked over her shoulder. There were dense, dark clouds gathering on the distant horizon. They needed rain, but not a storm.

Chapter 18

OCTOBER 28, 2042, 8:05 AM
SCOURGE +10 YEARS
DEL RIO, TEXAS

A lot of things go through a man's head when he's dying. Somewhere between the here and the hereafter, the fear and the pain dissolve into calm and acceptance.

Some say there's nothing but a black void in those precious final moments. Others talk about a bright light and a welcoming warmth. Still more suggest that all the dead people who once loved, or cared, or played a positive role in someone's life are gathered at the end of a tunnel, urging the person home. There's no telling what would have greeted Marcus Battle.

He never got that far. He never felt the calm or resigned himself to accepting what was coming. He fought it.

He fought to stay alive while Lou used everything she had in the first aid kit and everything she'd learned reading books about medicine to stop the bleeding. The shot was through and through and, remarkably, hit Marcus in almost the identical spot he'd been shot before. There was damage there and a real risk for infection. For now though, the immediate threat had passed.

Lou worked with speed and precision to stop the bleeding, clean the entry and exit wounds, and sew them shut. It wasn't the first time she'd tried stitching up torn flesh, but it was her first attempt on someone else. It was harder on another person, she found, especially since Marcus occasionally thrashed about and mumbled incoherently about things she'd never heard him mention before.

Pico. Rufus. Skinner.

After she'd stitched the injuries closed, she cleaned the skin again and then covered them with bandages. She used a rag to wipe his forehead free of the beads of sweat that dripped down his temples and into the corners of his eyes. His fever broke. His breathing slowed and regulated.

Lou had saved his life again.

When Marcus finally came to, the sun was rising again. He blinked his eyes open and tried moving to one side. He winced and reached for the wound at his side. Lou gently took his hand in hers and rested it on his chest.

Marcus focused and looked Lou in the eyes before laying his head back. He closed his eyes and winced again, air leaking from between his teeth.

"So what now?" Lou asked. She was sitting directly in front of him in a wooden chair. Fifty was at her side and she was rubbing his head.

Marcus opened his eyes again and adjusted his weight onto one side. He was in the oversized club chair. He looked around the room. Lou had dragged the bodies into the far corner. All five of the men were dead. There were flies buzzing around the open window. He licked his cracked, dry lips.

Lou handed him the canteen. "Here," she said. "This is what's left of it."

Marcus took the water and gulped it from the canteen. Then he held the opening above his mouth and shook the remaining droplets from it. He set the canteen in his lap and noticed he was shirtless. There was a large blood-soaked bandage on his side.

Lou glanced at the wound. "I did my best. You can only learn so much from a book. I don't think the stitches are very good, at least not on the front. On your back I did a decent job."

Marcus didn't recognize his own voice when he spoke. It was raspy and hoarse. "Thank you. I guess this makes you the Wizard."

Lou smiled and shook her head. "No," she said. "The Wizard was a poseur. I'm the real deal."

Marcus chuckled and then winced from the sudden sting of pain at his side. "That you are."

"Who's Pico?" she asked. "Or Rufus? Or Skinner?"

Marcus swallowed hard. "How do you know about them?"

Lou shrugged. "You talked about them when you were unconscious. I couldn't understand much other than their names and a few other words."

"They're—" Marcus paused as he considered the best way to describe them "—all dead."

"I figured that much," Lou said. "Everyone you know is dead. I mean, except me and Rudy."

"That's true," said Marcus. "I have that effect on people. Spend enough time with me and you end up dead."

"Were they friends?"

Marcus shook his head. "No."

"Oh." Lou said. She stood, walked over to the window, and leaned against the sill.

The light from outside framed her thin silhouette. Her T-shirt hung on her body; her pants were cinched at her waist and gathered in a puddle at her shoes. Standing there for several minutes, she looked every bit the young girl she was. She spun the hat around on her head and crossed the room back to Marcus.

"So you didn't answer me," Lou said.

"I did," said Marcus. "I told you they weren't friends."

Lou shook her head. "No, I mean the other question. The one I asked first."

Marcus raised an eyebrow and leaned his head forward, silently asking for clarification.

"What now?" she asked again. "You got your revenge. All three of the men you wanted to kill, plus about a million others who got in your way, are dead. Are you going home?"

Home.

The word stung. It was if that four-letter word carried with it the disease that offed two-thirds of the world's population. *Home* left him alone for half a decade before it drew him into the wilderness, only to leave him abandoned again. *Home* was the thing he'd done so much to protect. *Home* was the thing that revealed so many of his failings.

Home.

It was a mythical place for imaginary people.

Marcus sank into the chair, gripping the threadbare arms. "I don't have a home," he said, his voice cracking.

Lou's eyes welled with tears and Marcus averted his, staring at the pile of bodies in the corner. The sight of those bodies was more familiar, almost more comforting to Marcus than anything else in his Godforsaken world.

"I think I'm going back to Abilene," he said. "They need help there. Maybe I could help."

Lou puffed her cheeks and exhaled. "Well, I know what's next for me."

Marcus's eyes narrowed underneath a knitted brow.

"I've got to return Fifty," she said. "He's only on loan, remember? Rudy's expecting him back."

"You're headed to Baird, then?"

"Baird."

"Baird isn't that far from Abilene," said Marcus.

Lou shrugged. "Practically the same town."

"We could head that way together."

"Like Dorothy and the Scarecrow," said Lou.

"Not the Tin Man?"

"I have a heart."

"Not the Lion?"

"I think I've proven I have courage."

"So you're saying you don't have a brain," Marcus said, changing his position in the chair to take the pressure off his lower back.

"No," Lou said, her face lighting up, "you're the Scarecrow, Marcus. You were always the Scarecrow."

Marcus scratched his beard against the growing irritation on his neck. He really needed a shave. "I thought I was Dorothy."

"Dorothy's the hero, Marcus, so that rules you out."

Lou stood from her seat and gently slid into the oversized chair next to Marcus. She laid her head on his shoulder. Marcus leaned his cheek on the top of her head, feeling the fabric of her Astros cap against his skin.

"I bet you were a good dad," said Lou.

"I know you were a good daughter," said Marcus.

"I'm glad I didn't kill you."

Marcus closed his eyes. "I'm glad you didn't kill me too, Dorothy. To be honest, I hope we're done killing for a while."

Lou yawned. "Me too, Marcus, but we both know that's not likely. We got a long road to Baird. We're bound to run into some obstacles along the way. Besides, sometimes people just need killin'."

Marcus sat there while the little philosopher named Lou fell asleep next to him. There was blood on her fingers, painting her cuticles and nails. It was his blood. Or maybe it wasn't. She was as much a killer as he.

She was right. They lived in a world where violence was law and evil ruled. A black bird fluttered its wings outside the window and perched on the sill. It pecked its head toward the bodies and then at Marcus, its black eyes staring through him.

Marcus stared back at the bird. It cocked its head and rocked on its small feet before flapping its wings and darting from the sill to the outside. A minute later it was back with a second bird. A third appeared at the sill. They were apparently biding their time.

Marcus watched the birds pace back and forth until one of them had the gumption to hop to the floor and skitter to the bodies. A second joined. So did the third.

While Lou snored loudly against Marcus's shoulder, the trio grew bolder and pecked at their would-be meal. The pecking quickly became more aggressive and Marcus wondered if perhaps all of the killing had purpose. In *that* purpose he believed he could find his own.

In the end, in some small way, he *could* be more than a soldier, a failed protector, a crazed killer, or a revenge-seeking vigilante.

He could be the hero.

COMING IN LATE 2017

BATTLE: THE TRAVELER SERIES PART FIVE

Read an Excerpt from *Battle*

"I'm getting too old for this," Marcus Battle muttered under his breath.

He wiggled his fingers above the grip of his Glock at his hip. His feet were shoulder width apart on the cracked, hole-riddled asphalt and he straddled what was left of the faded double yellow line that ran through town. Despite the dry chill of a late West Texas winter, Marcus was in short sleeves. Sweat coated the back of his neck and under his arms.

His muscled tensed and his focus sharpened on the target standing thirty yards from him in the street. He drew slow, even breaths.

"You're the one they used to call Mad Max," sneered the target. "I heard tell of you all over the territory south of the wall."

Marcus didn't respond. He leaned forward at his hips, positioning his shoulders over his toes. It was the best position from which to fire his weapon.

"They say you ended the Cartel single-handedly," said the target, "turned your back on the Dwellers, got north of the wall, and came back to kill most of the Llano River Clan."

The target had the story mostly right. There was a defiance in the man's voice. There was also fear. Marcus could hear it as the man recounted the dime store tales of Marcus Battle's violent adventures. He was the most recent in a long succession of would-be sharks who'd circled Baird before diving into its waters in hopes of besting its legendary Sheriff.

Marcus wasn't really the Sheriff. There wasn't such a thing south of the wall in the territory once known as Texas. But he'd found people to lead in the town of Baird. They'd wanted his help and he'd given it freely.

For six months it had been easy. Word hadn't gotten out. Then it did. Things changed. Now, almost weekly, some young gun or guns came calling. They called out Marcus by name or reputation and demanded the chance to seek out glory.

This was one tall and thin. His arms were almost comically long and his sleeves stopped short of his wrists. His baggy pants ended at his calves. "I also heard you ain't got no family," said the target, smiling as he spoke. "And you're here 'cause your home is gone. They say you got nowhere to go and nobody to go to, so you're here. That's pathetic, if you ask me."

At first Marcus had tried to talk them out of their mission, to offer them refuge from the violence and unease that plagued the lawless, wild south. None of them accepted. They insisted. One by one they'd failed in their quest and Marcus had buried them himself a mile outside of town. Marcus fingers had blistered then thickened with callouses from the frequency of the work.

The target widened his stance. His hand still hovered above the holster at his side. "I used to believe what they say," he shouted. "I used to believe the stories. I thought you were a giant full of muscles."

Here stood another one. Another body to put in the ground, Marcus thought. He rubbed the side of his thumb against his twitchy trigger finger.

"You don't look so tough," said the target. "You look old. I ain't impressed one b—"

The nine millimeter bullet drilled through the center of the challenger's forehead and exploded out the back of his head before he could finish his sentence. Marcus already had the Glock back in his holster and snapped shut by the time the silenced target went limp and collapsed the ground face first. His mouth was still open int he shape of a "B" when his brain stopped working and his heart stopped. He hadn't drawn his weapon.

"That was anti-climactic," said Lou. She was leaning against the brick facade of a building to Marcus's right. "You didn't let him complete his thought."

Marcus sighed and scratched his beard. It was time to shave again. "I'd heard enough," he said and closed the distance to Lou. "I half expected you to put a blade in him before I had a chance to fire."

Lou curled her lips into a pout and shrugged. She put a hand on one of the knives in her waistband. "I considered it," she thought. "He *was* a talkative one."

Marcus stepped up the curb onto the wide cement sidewalk that separated the street from the long rows of buildings that lined both sides of the main boulevard that ran through the center of Baird. From the look of the place it could have been 1894 as easily as it was 2044.

Marcus leaned against the building next to Lou. "Just once," he said, "I'd like for these punks to take me up on my offer of sanctuary, forgiven transgressions, et cetera. They're too stubborn, too confident in their own abilities."

"Yeah," Lou said, folding her arms across her chest, "but they only have to be better than you once You have to be better than them every time."

Marcus rubbed his aching neck, digging his thumb into a knot below the back of his head. Lou was right. It only took one hot shot with a quicker draw, or one who decided to snipe him without warning.

He nudged Lou with his shoulder. "Let's hope that's later rather than sooner," he said. "You gonna help me with the body?"

Acknowledgments

Immeasurable gratitude always begins with Courtney, Sam, and Luke. You're my everything.

A big thanks to Felicia A. Sullivan, who edited my work from the beginning. She's one in a million.

Thanks also to Pauline Nolet and Patricia Wilson for their proofing talent. They catch everything. And to Stef McDaid for giving the book a terrifically professional look.

Cover artist Hristo Kovatliev is a master at his craft and is so patient when I ask for tweaks and changes.

To Kevin Pierce, who provides the voice for this series in the audiobook format, I am grateful we connected and have together to create this world. You *are* Marcus Battle.

Steve Kremer provided excellent help with the early manuscript. Thank you.

And I thank my parents, Sanders and Jeanne, my siblings, Penny and Steven, and my mother-in-law, Linda Eaker, for undying support and encouragement.

Lastly, thanks to all of you readers who demanded a return of Marcus Battle. He lives because of you.

Made in the USA
Middletown, DE
29 March 2019